The Old Man and the Sea
Abridged From the Originel Novel
老人與海（原著刪節版）

Let's Enjoy Masterpieces!

All the beautiful fairy tales and masterpieces that you have encountered during your childhood remain as warm memories in your adulthood. This time, let's indulge in the world of masterpieces through English. You can enjoy the depth and beauty of original works, which you can't enjoy through Chinese translations.

The stories are easy for you to understand because of your familiarity with them. When you enjoy reading, your ability to understand English will also rapidly improve.

This series of *Let's Enjoy Masterpieces* are a special reading comprehension booster program, devised to improve reading comprehension for beginners whose command of English is not satisfactory, or who are elementary, middle, and high school students. With this program, you can enjoy reading masterpieces in English with fun and efficiency.

This carefully planned program is composed of 5 levels, from the beginner level of 350 words to the intermediate and advanced levels of 1,000 words. With this program's level-by-level system, you are able to read famous texts in English and to savor the true pleasure of the world's language.

The program is well conceived, composed of reader-friendly explanations of English expressions and grammar, quizzes to help the student learn vocabulary and understand the meaning of the texts, and fabulous illustrations that adorn every page. In addition, with our "Guide to Listening," not only is reading comprehension enhanced but also listening comprehension skills are highlighted.

In the audio recording of the book, texts are vividly read by professional American actors. The texts are rewritten, according to the levels of the readers by an expert editorial staff of native speakers, on the basis of standard American English with the ministry of education recommended vocabulary. Therefore, it will be of great help even for all the students that want to learn English.

Please indulge yourself in the fun of reading and listening to English through *Let's Enjoy Masterpieces*.

Introduction

海明威
Ernest Hemingway (1899-1961)

Ernest Hemingway was an American novelist from Illinois. His earliest short stories, published in his high school newspaper, demonstrated his gift for storytelling. After graduation from high school, he decided to skip college and got a job working for a local newspaper as a journalist.

In 1918, Hemingway joined the Red Cross to participate in World War One. He was wounded on the Italian front and came back home. He then went to Europe as a foreign correspondent. While in Europe, Hemingway spent time with many famous writers, and he continued to write.

In 1923, his first book, *Three Short Stories and Ten Poems* was published. *A Farewell to Arms*, which came out in 1929, was essential to gaining him his literary reputation as a novelist. Published in 1952, *The Old Man and the Sea*, which describes an old fisherman's lonely struggle to catch a giant fish, received great critical acclaim. This novel was awarded the 1953 Pulitzer Prize and the Nobel Prize for Literature in 1954.

Ernest Hemingway died in July 1961. His death from a gunshot wound was considered to be a suicide. Hemingway is regarded as one of the 20th century's greatest writers.

The Old Man and the Sea exemplifies the spirit in life that Hemingway admired, described, and pursued. The story is about an old fisherman who finally catches a giant marlin after weeks of not catching anything. However, sailing homeward with the fish, he encounters sharks that devour the marlin's meat. By the time he returns to the harbor, only the skeleton of the fish is left.

This simple story's plot doesn't contain any big symbolism or great philosophy. Hemingway just vividly described a joyous triumph won in a relentless, agonizing battle, by using the story of an old man who would never cease his struggle. As the old man says in the book, "A man can be destroyed but not defeated." The old man naturally tries hard to keep the giant marlin he has hooked and his epic endeavor exemplifies Hemingway's ideal that indomitable courage is the eternal triumph of the human spirit.

With simple and powerful language, Hemingway depicted the spirit of the fisherman and the dynamics of life. *The Old Man and the Sea* is praised as a crowning achievement for best exhibiting Hemingway's belief that although your life is a fight and defeat is the ultimate outcome, the dignity you will win during your struggle is a triumph worthy of respect.

contents

Before You Read

Old Man

I have been a fisherman all my life. I am old now, but I am still strong and determined. I am a master fisherman. That means I have a lot of knowledge about how to catch a fish. However, I have not caught a fish for many weeks. I know that I will catch a fish soon. So I go out in my boat everyday and put out my fishing lines.

Boy

I live in Havana, near the beach with all the other fishermen. I learned how to fish when I was very young. The old man taught me everything I know about fishing. He is a great man, but my parents think he's unlucky. I believe he will catch a great fish again one day.

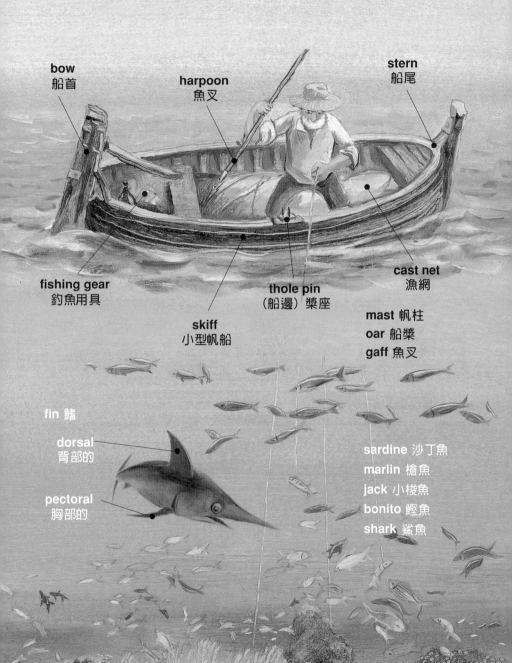

bow
船首

harpoon
魚叉

stern
船尾

fishing gear
釣魚用具

thole pin
（船邊）槳座

cast net
漁網

skiff
小型帆船

mast 帆柱
oar 船槳
gaff 魚叉

fin 鰭

dorsal
背部的

pectoral
胸部的

sardine 沙丁魚
marlin 槍魚
jack 小梭魚
bonito 鰹魚
shark 鯊魚

9

CHAPTER ONE

The Worst Kind of Luck

He was an old man who fished alone in a skiff[1] in the Gulf Stream[2] and he had gone eighty-four days without catching a fish. During the first forty days without a fish the boy's parents had told him that the old man was now definitely[3]

1. skiff [skɪf] (n.) 輕舟；小艇
2. the Gulf Stream
   墨西哥灣流
3. definitely [ˋdefɪnətli] (adv.)
   無疑地；確定地
4. gaff [gaf] (n.) 魚鉤
5. harpoon [hɑːrˋpuːn]
   (n.) 魚叉
6. patch [pætʃ] (v.)
   補釘；修補
7. flour sack 麵粉袋
8. furl [fɜːrl] (v.) 捲起
9. permanent [ˋpɜːrmənənt]
   (a.) 永恆的；永遠的
10. defeat [dɪˋfiːt] (n.)
    挫敗；戰敗

salao — the worst form of unlucky. The boy's parents had ordered him to go in another boat, which caught three good fish the first week. It made the boy sad to see the old man come back each day with his skiff empty. He always went down to help him carry the lines, or the gaff[4] and harpoon[5] and the sail patched[6] with flour sacks[7], so that when it was furled[8] it looked like the flag of permanent[9] defeat[10].

The old man was thin and gaunt[11] with deep wrinkles[12] on the back of his neck and deep scars on his hands from handling lines of heavy fish. The dark spots[13] of the benign[14] skin cancer[15] that the tropical[16] sun brings were on his cheeks. His scars were as old as forgotten memories.

Everything about him was old except his eyes. They were the same color as the sea and were cheerful and undefeated.

11. gaunt [gɔːnt] (a.) 消瘦的
12. wrinkle [ˋrɪŋkl] (n.) 皺紋
13. spot [spɑːt] (n.) 斑點
14. benign [bɪˋnaɪn] (a.) 良性的
15. cancer [ˋkænsə(r)] (n.) 腫瘤；癌
16. tropical [ˋtrɑːpɪkl] (a.) 熱帶的

"Santiago," the boy said
to him, "I could go with
you again. We've made
some money[1]." The old man had taught the boy
to fish and the boy loved him.
"No," the old man said. "You're with a lucky
boat. Stay there."
"But remember how you went eighty-seven
days without fish and then we caught[2] big ones
every day for three weeks."
"I remember," the old man said. "I know you did
not leave me because you doubted[3]."

1. make money 賺錢
2. catch [kætʃ] (v.) 捕獲
   (catch-caught-caught)
3. doubt [daʊt] (v.)
   懷疑；不相信
4. obey [əˋbeɪ] (v.)
   服從；聽話
5. faith [feɪθ] (n.) 信念；信任
6. offer [ˋɑːfə(r)] (v.)
   給予；提供
7. stuff [stʌf] (n.) 東西
8. take A home 帶 A 回家
9. Why not? 為什麼不呢？
10. between [bɪˋtwiːn]
    (prep.) 在……之間

"It was papa who made me leave.
I am a boy and I must obey[4] him."
"I know," the old man said.
"He hasn't much faith[5]."
"No, but we have. Haven't we?"
"Yes. Can I offer[6] you a beer on the Terrace
and then we'll take the stuff[7] home[8]."
"Why not[9]?" the old man said. "Between[10]
fishermen."

They sat on the Terrace and many of the fishermen made fun of[1] the old man, but he was not angry. The older fishermen looked at him and were sad, but they did not show it. The successful fishermen of that day had already butchered[2] their marlin[3] and carried them to the ice truck that would take them to the market in Havana[4]. Those who had caught sharks[5] had taken them to the shark factory on the other side of[6] the cove[7]. When the wind came from the East a smell came from the shark factory.

"Santiago," the boy said.
"Yes," the old man said. He was thinking of many years ago.

"Can I go out and get sardines[8] for you for tomorrow?"

"No. Go and play baseball. I can still row[9] and Rogelio will throw the net[10]."

"I would like to go. If I cannot fish with you, I would like to serve[11] in some way."

"You bought me a beer," the old man said. "You are already a man."

"How old was I when you first took me in a boat?"

"Five and you were nearly killed when I brought the fish in too green[12] and it nearly destroyed[13] the boat. Can you remember?"

1. make fun of 嘲弄；開玩笑
2. butcher [ˋbutʃə(r)] (v.) 屠宰
3. marlin [ˋmɑːrlɪn] (n.) 槍魚
4. Havana
   哈瓦那，古巴首都
5. shark [ʃɑːrk] (n.) 鯊魚
6. on the other side of . . .
   在……的另一邊
7. cove [koʊv] (n.)
   小灣；小港
8. sardine [ˌsɑːrˋdiːn]
   (n.) 沙丁魚
9. row [roʊ] (v.) 划（船）
10. throw/cast a net 撒網
11. serve [sɜːrv] (v.)
    服務；貢獻
12. in (too) green 時機未成熟
13. destroy [dɪˋstrɔɪ] (v.) 毀滅

"I can remember the tail slapping[1] and the noise of the clubbing[2]."

"Can you really remember that?"

"I remember everything from when we went together."

The old man looked at him with his confident[3], loving eyes. "If you were my boy I'd take you out," he said. "But you are your father's and your mother's and you are in a lucky boat."

"May I get the sardines? I know where I can get four baits[4] too. "

"I have mine left from today."

"Let me get four fresh ones."

"One," the old man said. His hope and his confidence had never left him.

---

1. slap [slæp] (v.) 拍擊
2. clubbing [klʌbɪŋ]
   (n.) 用棍棒打
3. confident [ˋkɑːnfɪdənt]
   (a.) 自信的
4. bait [beɪt] (n.) 餌
5. current [ˋkɜːrənt]
   (n.) 水流；潮流
6. attain [əˋteɪn] (v.) 獲得
7. humility [hjuːˋmɪləti]
   (n.) 謙遜
8. pride [praɪd] (n.)
   自負；自豪

16

"Two," the boy said.

"Two," the old man agreed. "You didn't steal them?"

"I would," the boy said. "But I bought these."

"Thank you," the old man said. "Tomorrow is going to be a good day with this current[5]."
He was too simple to wonder when he had attained[6] humility[7].
But he knew it carried no loss of pride[8].

"Where are you going?" the boy asked.
"Far out. I want to be out before it is light."

"Are you strong enough now for a truly big fish?"

"I think so. And there are many tricks[1]."

"Let us take the stuff home," the boy said. "So I can get the cast net and go after[2] the sardines."

They picked up the things from the boat. The old man carried the mast[3] on his shoulder[4] and the boy carried the wooden box with the fishing gear[5].

They walked to the old man's shack[6] and went in through its open door. The shack was made of the tough part of the royal palm[7] called *guano*.

In the shack there was a bed, a table, one chair and a place on the dirt[8] floor to cook with charcoal[9]. On the brown walls there was a color picture of the Sacred Heart of Jesus and another of the Virgin of Cobre, both relics[10] of his wife.

Once there had been a photograph of his wife on the wall but he had taken it down because it had made him lonely. Now it was on the shelf in the corner[11] under his clean shirt.

1. trick [trɪk] (n.) 技巧
2. go after 在……後面
3. mast [mæst] (n.) 桅杆
4. carry A on one's shoulder
   用肩扛著A
5. fishing gear 魚具
6. shack [ʃæk] (n.)
   簡陋的小屋
7. royal palm
   〔植〕大王椰子
8. dirt [dɜːrt] (n.) 灰塵；穢物
9. charcoal [ˋtʃɑːrkoʊl]
   (n.) 木炭
10. relic [ˋrelɪk] (n.)
    遺物；紀念物
11. in the corner 在角落

19

"What do you have to eat?" the boy asked.

"A pot of yellow rice with fish. Do you want some?"

"No. I will eat at home. Do you want me to make a fire¹?"

"No. I will make it later on."

"May I take the cast net?"

"Of course."

There was no cast net and the boy remembered when they had sold it. But they went through² this fiction³ every day. There was no pot of yellow rice and fish and the boy knew this too.

"Eighty-five is a lucky number," the old man said. "How would you like to see me bring one in that weighed⁴ over a thousand pounds?"

"I'll get the cast net and go for sardines. Will you sit in the sun in the doorway⁵?"

1. make a fire 生火
2. go through 經歷
3. fiction [ˈfɪkʃn] (n.)
   虛構；謊言
4. weigh [weɪ] (v.)
   重……重量

5. doorway [ˈdɔːrweɪ]
   (n.) 門口
6. paper [ˈpeɪpə(r)] (n.) 報紙
7. bring [brɪŋ] (v.) 拿來
   (bring-brought-brought)

20

"Yes. I have yesterday's paper and I will read about baseball."

The boy did not know whether yesterday's paper[6] was fiction too. But the old man brought[7] it out from under the bed.
"Perico gave it to me at the bodega[8]," he explained.

"I'll be back when I have the sardines.
I'll keep yours and mine together on ice and we can share[9] them in the morning. When I come back you can tell me about baseball.
Now keep warm[10] old man. Remember we are in September," the boy said.

"The month when the great fish come," the old man said. "Anyone can be a fisherman in May."
"I'm going for[11] the sardines now," the boy said.

8. bodega 酒店
9. share [ʃer] (v.) 分享
10. keep warm 保暖
11. go for . . . 前往……

When the boy came back the old man was asleep[1] in the chair and the sun was down[2]. The boy took the old army blanket[3] off the bed and spread it over[4] the back of the chair and over the old man's strange but powerful shoulders.

His shirt had been patched[5] so many times that it was like a sail[6]. The old man's head was very old and with his eyes closed there was no life in his face. He was barefoot[7].

1. asleep [əˋsliːp] (a.) 睡著的
2. the sun is down
   太陽已經下山
3. army blanket 軍毯
4. spread A over B
   把 A 鋪在 B 上
5. patch [pætʃ] (v.)
   補釘；修補

The boy left him there and when he came back
the old man was still asleep.

"Wake up[8] old man," the boy said.
The old man opened his eyes[9] and for a
moment[10] he was coming back from[11]
a longway away.
 Then he smiled.
"What have you got?" he asked.
"Supper," said the boy. "We're going to have
supper."
"I'm not very hungry."
"Come on and eat. You can't fish and not eat."
"What are we eating?"
"Black beans[12] and rice,
fried bananas and some stew."

6. sail [seɪl] (n.) 帆布
7. barefoot [ˋberfʊt]
   (a.) 赤足的
8. wake up 起床；醒過來
9. open one's eyes 張開眼睛

10. for a moment 片刻間
11. come back from . . .
    從……回來
12. bean [biːn] (n.) 豆子；豆類

The boy had brought[1] them in a metal container[2] from the Terrace.

"That's very kind of you," the old man said. "Should we eat?"

"I've been asking you to," the boy told him gently. "I didn't want to open the container until you were ready[3]."

"I'm ready now," the old man said. "I only needed time to wash."

"Where did he wash?" the boy thought. The village water supply[4] was two streets down the road. I must have water here for him, and soap and a towel. Why am I so thoughtless[5]? I must get him another shirt and a jacket for the winter and some sort of shoes and another blanket. "Your stew is excellent," the old man said.

1. bring [brɪŋ] (v.) 帶來
2. metal container 金屬容器
3. ready [ˋrɛdi] (a.) 準備好的
4. water supply 供水
5. thoughtless [ˋθɔːtləs]
   (a.) 欠考慮的；粗心的
6. lose [luːz] (v.) 輸；失敗
7. oneself [wʌnˋsɛlf]
   (pron.) 自己；本人
8. make a difference
   使區別；使不同
9. used to . . . 過去時常……

"Tell me about baseball," the boy asked him.

"In the American League it is the Yankees as I said," the old man said happily.

"They lost[6] today," the boy told him.

"That means nothing. The great DiMaggio is himself[7] again."

"They have other men on the team."

"Naturally. But he makes the difference[8]," the old man said. "Do you remember when he used to[9] come to the Terrace? I wanted to take him fishing[10] but I was too timid[11] to ask him. Then I asked you to ask him and you were too timid. I would like to take the great DiMaggio fishing. They say his father was a fisherman. Maybe he was as poor as[12] we are and would understand."

"I used to sail on a big ship that went to Africa and I have seen lions on the beaches in the evening."

"I know. You told me."

10. take A fishing 帶 A 去釣魚
11. timid [ˈtɪmɪd] (a.)
　　膽小的；膽怯的
12. as poor as . . .
　　和⋯⋯一樣貧窮

"Should we talk about Africa or about baseball?"

"Baseball. Tell me about the great John Jota McGraw," the boy said.

"He used to come to the Terrace sometimes in the older days[1]. But he was rough and harsh-spoken[2] when he drank[3] too much."

"Who is the greatest manager[4], really, Luque or Mike Gonzalez?"

"I think they are equal[5]."

"And the best fisherman is you."

"No. I know others that are better."

1. in the older days
   在過去的日子裡
2. harsh-spoken 言辭粗糙
3. drink [drɪŋk] (v.) 喝酒
   (drink-drank-drunk)
4. manager [ˈmænɪdʒə(r)] (n.)
   經理；經紀人
5. equal [ˈiːkwəl] (a.) 同等的
6. Que va
   你說的是什麼話啊！
   (= What are you saying!)
7. prove [pruːv] (v.) 證明
8. resolution [ˌrezəˈluːʃn]
   (n.) 決心

"*Qué va*[6]," the boy said, "There are many good fishermen and some great ones, but there is only you."

"Thank you. You make me happy. I hope no fish will come along so great that he will prove[7] us wrong."

"There is no such fish if you are still strong as you say."

"I may not be as strong as I think," the old man said. "But I know many tricks and I have resolution[8]."

"You ought to¹ go to bed now so that you will be
fresh² in the morning."
"Good night then.
I will wake you in the morning."
"You're my alarm clock³," the boy said.

1. ought to 應該要
2. fresh [freʃ] (a.)
   有朝氣的；清新的
3. alarm clock 鬧鐘
4. sleep late and hard
   睡得很晚很熟
5. with no light 沒有燈光
6. roll up 捲起來

"Age is my alarm clock," the old man said.
"Why do old men wake so early?
Is it to have longer days?"

"I don't know," the boy said. "All I know is that young boys sleep late and hard[4]. Sleep well, old man."

They had eaten with no light[5] on the table. The old man rolled[6] his trousers[7] up to make a pillow[8], putting the newspaper inside them. He rolled himself in the blanket[9] and slept on the other old newspapers that covered[10] the springs[11] of the bed.

7. trousers ['traʊzərz]
   (n.) 長褲
8. pillow ['pɪloʊ] (n.) 枕頭
9. roll oneself in the blanket
   把自己捲在毯子裡

10. cover ['kʌvə(r)] (v.) 覆蓋
11. spring [sprɪŋ] (n.) 彈簧

Hemingway and "The Old Man and the Sea"

When Hemingway wrote "The Old Man and the Sea," he was an old man himself. His previous novel was not a good book. But "The Old Man and the Sea" was instantly a huge success. The simple, clear language Hemingway used to describe an old man's determination to succeed one more time appealed to many readers all over the world. Some people think that Hemingway was writing about himself, as a writer who wanted one more big success.

Many other people believe Hemingway based the character on Gregorio Fuentes, a Cuban who worked for the author. Fuentes was the captain of Hemingway's fishing boat, the Pilar, when Hemingway lived in Cuba.

However, Fuentes once told a reporter a different story. One day he and Hemingway were sailing on the Pilar when they saw an old fisherman. This man was in a small boat and had a large fish tied to the side. Hemingway told Fuentes he wanted to write about the fisherman.

Perhaps Hemingway combined parts of himself, his friends and people he saw to create the main character. After all, that could be why the story appeals to so many readers: the old man represents all men who struggle, determined to win just one more time.

CHAPTER TWO

Far Out to Sea

The old man dreamed of[1] Africa when he was a boy and the long, golden beaches. He lived along that coast[2] now every night and in his dreams he heard the surf[3] roar[4] and saw the native[5] boats come riding through[6] it. As he slept he smelled the smell of Africa that the land breeze[7] brought in the morning.

1. dream of 夢見
2. coast [koʊst] (n.) 海岸
3. surf [sɜːrf] (n.) 浪花
4. roar [rɔː(r)] (v.) 呼嘯；怒號
5. native [ˈneɪtɪv] (a.) 當地的
6. ride through
   乘著⋯⋯航行
7. breeze [briːz] (n.) 微風
8. contest of strength 比腕力
9. in the dusk 在黃昏

He no longer dreamed of storms, nor of women, nor of great events, nor of great fish, nor fights, nor contests of strength[8], nor of his wife. Now he only dreamed of places and of the lions on the beach. They played like young cats in the dusk[9] and he loved them as he loved the boy. He never dreamed about the boy.

He woke up, looked out the open door at the moon and unrolled[10] his trousers and put them on[11]. He went up the road to wake the boy. The door of the house where the boy lived was unlocked[12] and the old man opened it and walked in quietly. He took hold of[13] the boy's foot gently and held it until the boy woke and turned and looked at him. The old man nodded[14] and the boy took his trousers from the chair by the bed and, sitting on the bed, pulled them on[15].

---

10. unroll [ʌn`roʊl]
    (v.) 攤開；展開
11. put on 穿上
12. unlocked [ʌn`lɑ:kt]
    (a.) 沒有鎖的

13. take hold of 握住
14. nod [nɑ:d] (v.) 點頭
15. pull on 拉上

The old man went out the door and the boy came after[1] him. He was sleepy and the old man put his arm across his shoulders[2] and said, "I am sorry."

"*Qué va*," the boy said.

"It is what a man must do."

They walked down the road to the old man's shack and all along the road, in the dark, barefoot men were moving, carrying the masts[3] of their boats.

1. come after 跟在後面
2. put one's arm across the shoulders
   用手臂環住肩膀
3. mast [mæst] (n.) 帆柱
4. roll [roʊl] (n.) 捲；綑
5. gaff [gæf] (n.) 大魚鈎
6. furled [fɜːrl] (a.)
   捲起的；摺起的
7. gear [gɪr] (n.) 工具

When they reached the old man's shack the boy took the rolls[4] of line in the basket, the harpoon and gaff[5], and the old man carried the mast with the furled[6] sail on his shoulder.

"Do you want coffee?" the boy asked.

"We'll put the gear[7] in the boat and then get some."

They had coffee from condensed-milk[8] cans at an early morning place that served[9] fishermen.

"How did you sleep old man?" the boy asked. He was waking up now although[10] it was still hard for him to leave his sleep[11].

8. condensed-milk 煉乳
9. serve [sɜːrv] (v.)
   服務；招待（顧客）
10. although [ɔːlˈðoʊ] (conj.)
    雖然；儘管
11. leave one's sleep
    離開夢鄉

"Very well, Manolin," the old man said.
"I feel confident today."
"So do I," the boy said. "Now I must get your
sardines and mine and your fresh baits."
"I'll be right back," the boy said. "Have another
coffee. We have credit[1] here."

The old man drank his coffee slowly. It was all
he would have all day and he knew that he
should drink it. For a long time[2] now eating had
bored[3] him and he never carried a lunch[4].
He had a bottle of water in the bow[5] of the skiff
and that was all he needed for the day.

The boy was back now with the sardines and
the two baits, and they went down to the skiff,
feeling the pebbled sand[6] under their feet[7].
They lifted the skiff and slid her into[8] the water.

1. have credit 允許賒帳
2. for a long time
   長久以來
3. bore [bɔː(r)] (v.) 使無趣
4. carry a lunch 帶著午餐
5. bow [baʊ] (n.) 船首
6. pebbled sand
   粗糙帶著小石頭的沙灘
7. feel A under one's feet
   感覺 A 在腳下
8. slide A into 把 A 滑進……
9. fit [fɪt] (v.) 調整；配合

"Good luck, old man."

"Good luck," the old man said.

He fitted[9] the rope lashings[10] of the oars[11] onto the thole pins[12] and, leaning forward[13], he began to row out of the harbor in the dark.

There were other boats going out to sea and the old man heard the dip[14] and push of their oars even though[15] he could not see them.

10. lashing [ˈlæʃɪŋ] (n.) 捆綁
11. oar [ɔ:(r)] (n.) 船槳
12. thole pin （船邊的）槳架

13. lean forward 往前傾靠
14. dip [dɪp] (n.) 下沈；傾斜
15. even though 即使；雖然

The old man knew he was going far out[1] and he left the smell of the land behind[2] and rowed out into the clean early morning smell of the ocean.

In the dark the old man could feel the morning coming and as he rowed he heard the sound of flying fish[3] leaving the water. He was very fond of[4] flying fish as they were his principal friends[5] on the ocean. He was sorry for the birds, especially the small delicate[6] dark terns[7] that were always flying and looking and almost never finding. And he thought, "The birds have a harder life than we do except for the robber[8] birds and the heavy strong ones. Why did they make birds so delicate and fine[9] as those sea swallows when the ocean can be so cruel? She is kind and very beautiful. But she can be so cruel[10]."

1. go far out 前往遠處
2. leave A behind
   把 A 拋在後方
3. flying fish 飛魚
4. be fond of 高興
5. principal friend
   重要的朋友
6. delicate [ˋdelɪkət] (a.)
   精巧的；纖細的
7. tern [tɝn] (n.) 燕鷗
   (= sea swallow)
8. robber [ˋrɑːbə(r)] (n.) 盜匪
9. fine [faɪn] (a.) 細緻的
10. cruel [kruːəl] (a.) 殘酷的
11. masculine [ˋmæskjəlɪn]
    (a.) 男性的；剛強的
12. contestant [kənˋtestənt]
    (n.) 競爭對手

He always thought of the sea as *la mar* which is what people call her in Spanish when they love her. Sometimes those who love her say bad things about her but they always speak of the sea as though she were a woman. Some of the younger fishermen, who had motor-boats, speak of her as *el mar* which is masculine[11]. They speak of her as a contestant[12] or a place or even as an enemy.

But the old man always thought of her as feminine[13] and as something that gave or withheld[14] great favors[15], and if she did wild or wicked[16] things it was because she could not help them. The moon affects her as it does a woman, he thought.

13. feminine [ˈfemənɪn]
    (n.) 女性
14. withhold [wɪθˈhould]
    (v.) 保留；抑制
15. favor [ˈfeɪvə(r)] (n.)
    偏愛；偏袒
16. wicked [ˈwɪkɪd] (a.) 邪惡的

He was rowing steadily[1] and it was no effort for him.

"Today I'll row out where the schools[2] of bonito[3] and albacore[4] are and maybe there will be a big one with them."

Before it was really light he had his four baits out at different depths[5] and he was drifting[6] with the current. There was no part of the hook that a great fish could feel which was not sweet-smelling and good tasting.

The boy had given him two small fresh tunas which hung[7] on the two deepest lines and, on the others, he had a big blue runner[8] and a yellow jack[9].
Each line was as thick as a big pencil and was looped[10] onto a stick so that any pull or touch on the bait would make the stick dip[11].
Now the old man rowed gently to keep the lines straight[12] and at their proper depths.

1. **steadily** [ˈstedəli] (adv.)
   平穩地；穩定地
2. **school** [skuːl] (n.) （魚）群
3. **bonito** 鰹魚
4. **albacore** 青花魚

5. **at different depths**
   不同深度
6. **drift** [drɪft] (v.) 漂；漂流
7. **hang** [hæŋ] (v.) 勾；掛
   (hang-hung-hung)

The sun rose thinly from the sea and the old man could see the other boats, low on the water and well in toward the shore.

He looked down into the water and watched the lines that went straight down into the dark water. He kept them straighter than any other fisherman.

"I keep them with precision[13]," he thought. "Only I have no luck anymore." But who knows? Maybe today. Every day is a new day. It is better to be lucky. But I would rather be exact. Then when luck comes you are ready.

Just then he saw a man-of-war bird[14] with his long black wings circling[15] in the sky ahead of him. He made a quick drop[16] and then circled again.

8. blue runner 藍色參科魚
9. jack [dʒæk] (n.) 小梭魚
10. loop [luːp] (v.) 環繞；捲起
11. dip [dɪp] (v.)
　　下沉；向下傾斜
12. keep straight 維持直的

13. with precision 維持精確度
14. man-of-war bird 軍艦鳥
15. circle [sɜːrkl] (v.) 繞圈
16. drop [drɑːp] (n.)
　　落下；驟降

"He's got something," the old man said aloud[1].
"He's not just looking."
"Dolphin," the old man said aloud.
"Big dolphin."

As the old man watched, a small tuna rose in
the air[2], turned and dropped[3] into the water.
Another and another rose and they were
leaping[4] in long jumps after the bait.
After a while the stern[5] line became taut[6] under
his foot.

He dropped his oars and felt the weight[7] of the
small tuna's shivering[8] pull. He could see the
blue back of the fish in the water as he pulled
it in. The old man hit him on the head[9] for
kindness and kicked him under the stern.

1. aloud [ə`laʊd] (adv.)
   高聲地;響亮地
2. rise in the air 升至空中
   (rise-rose-risen)
3. drop [drɑːp] (v.)
   落下;降下
4. leap [liːp] (v.) 跳躍

5. stern [stɜːrn] (n.) 船尾
6. taut [tɔːt] (a.) 拉緊的
7. weight [weɪt] (n.) 重量
8. shiver [`ʃɪvə(r)] (v.)
   搖擺;振動
9. hit A on the head
   擊打 A 的頭

"Albacore[1]," he said aloud. "He'll make[2] a beautiful bait."

He did not remember when he first started talking to himself[3]. Probably when the boy had left him, but he did not remember.

The sun was hot now and the old man felt it on the back of his neck, and felt the sweat trickle down[4] his back as he rowed. Just then, watching his lines, he saw one of the projecting[5] green sticks dip sharply[6].

1. albacore 青花魚
2. make [meɪk] (v.) 使；形成
3. talk to oneself 對自己說話
4. trickle down 滴下
5. projecting [ˈprɑːdʒektɪŋ] (a.) 拋出的；凸出的
6. sharply [ˈʃɑːrpli] (adv.) 猛烈地；激烈地
7. reach out for 伸手去拿
8. delicately [ˈdelɪkətli] (adv.) 技巧精細地
9. thumb [θʌm] (n.) 大拇指

"Yes," he said. "Yes," and he moved his oars inside the boat. He reached out for[7] the line and held it delicately[8] between the thumb[9] and forefinger[10] of his right hand.

Then it came again. This time it was a tentative[11] pull and he knew exactly what it was. One hundred fathoms[12] below a marlin[13] was eating the sardines that covered the point[14] of the hook.

This far out, he must be huge, he thought. Eat them, fish. Please eat them. He felt the light delicate pull and then a harder pull when a sardine's head must have[15] been more difficult to break from the hook. Then there was nothing.

10. forefinger [ˈfɔːrfɪŋɡə(r)] (n.) 食指
11. tentative [ˈtentətɪv] (a.) 遲疑的；不確定的
12. fathom [ˈfæðəm] (n.) 噚，測水深的單位，一噚為六呎
13. marlin [ˈmɑːrlɪn] (n.) 槍魚
14. point [pɔɪnt] (n.) 尖端
15. must have + p.p. 想必，對過去的行為做推測

"Come on," the old man said aloud. "Just smell them. Aren't they lovely? Eat them now and then there is the tuna. Don't be shy, fish. Eat them."

Then he felt something hard and unbelievably heavy. It was the weight[1] of the fish and he let the line slip down[2], down, down. Now he was ready. He had three forty-fathom coils[3] of line in reserve[4], as well as[5] the coil he was using. "Eat it a little more," he said. "Eat it well." Eat it so that the point of the hook goes into your heart and kills you, he thought. Come up easy and let me put the harpoon into you. Are you ready? Have you been at the table[6] long enough?

"Now!" he said aloud and struck[7] hard with both hands, gained a yard of line and then struck again and again, swinging with all the strength of his arms and the weight of his body.

1. weight [weɪt] (n.) 重量
2. slip down 往下滑
3. coil [kɔɪl] (n.) 一圈；一捲
4. in reserve 保留；預備
5. as well as 而且；也
6. at the table 吃飯
7. strike [straɪk] (v.) 攻擊 (strike-struck-struck)
8. an inch 一英吋
9. tow [tou] (v.) 拖；拉

Nothing happened. The fish just moved away slowly and the old man could not raise him an inch[8]. The boat began to move slowly toward the northwest. The fish moved steadily and they traveled slowly on the calm water.

"I wish I had the boy," the old man said aloud. "I'm being towed[9] by a fish. I must hold him all I can and give him the line when he wants it. Thank God he is traveling and not going down."

Four hours later the fish was still swimming out to sea, towing the skiff, and the old man was still braced[10] solidly[11] with the line across his back.

10. brace [breɪs] (v.) 拉緊
11. solidly [ˈsɑːlɪdli] (adv.)
    有力地；堅固地

Comprehension Quiz

A True or False.

❶ The old man was deeply pessimistic. ☐T ☐F

❷ The old man lived on his fishing boat. ☐T ☐F

❸ The old man was having a streak of bad luck. ☐T ☐F

❹ The boy used to be the old man's apprentice. ☐T ☐F

❺ The boy lived with the old man. ☐T ☐F

❻ The old man usually dreams of his dead wife and lions. ☐T ☐F

B Rewrite the sentences with future continuous tense.

> The boy *helped* the old man get ready for the day's fishing.
>
> ⇨ The boy *will be helping* the old man get ready for the day's fishing.

❶ The old man hooked a huge fish.

⇨ _____

❷ The old man rowed far out to sea.

⇨ _____

❸ The tuna fish jumped out of the water.

⇨ _____

C Rearrange the following sentences in chronological order.

1. The old man caught a tuna fish.

2. The old man and the boy drank coffee together.

3. A big fish ate the old man's bait.

4. The old man's boat is towed far out to sea.

5. The old man rowed far from land.

_____ ⇨ _____ ⇨ _____ ⇨ _____ ⇨ _____

D Fill in the blanks with the given words.

> made   trousers   dream   taut   current

1. The old man rolled up his _____.

2. When the fish ate the hook, the line became _____.

3. Tomorrow is going to be a good day to fish with this _____.

4. The boy's father _____ him fish in another boat.

5. At night, the old man would _____ of Africa.

CHAPTER THREE

The Battle¹ Begins ③

He looked behind² him and saw that no land was visible³. That makes no difference⁴, he thought. I can always come in on the glow⁵ from Havana. Maybe he will come up before sunset, or with the moon.

I have no cramps⁶ and I feel strong. It is he that has the hook in his mouth.

1. battle [ˈbætl] (n.) 戰役
2. look behind 往後看
3. visible [ˈvɪzəbl] (a.) 可見的
4. make no difference
   沒什麼影響
5. glow [gloʊ] (n.) 熾熱；光輝
6. cramp [kræmp] (n.)
   抽筋；痙攣
7. against [əˈgeɪnst] (prep.)
   面對；與……競爭
8. course [kɔːrs] (n.)
   路線；方向

But what a fish to pull like that. I wish I could see him only once to know what I have against[7] me.

The fish never changed his course[8]. It was cold after the sun went down. He tied the sack[9] that covered the bait box around his neck so that it hung down[10] over his back and he cautiously[11] worked it down under the line that was across his shoulders now.

I can do nothing with him and he can do nothing with me, he thought. Once he stood up and urinated[12] over the side of the skiff and looked at the stars and checked his course. They were moving more slowly now and the glow of Havana was not so strong, so he knew the current must be carrying them eastward[13].

---

9. sack [sæk] (n.) 袋
10. hang down 懸；掛
11. cautiously [ˋkɔːʃəsli] (adv.) 留心地；注意地

12. urinate [ˋjurəneɪt] (v.) 小便
13. eastward [ˋiːstwərdz] (adv.) 向東方地

I wonder how the baseball came out[1] in the grand leagues[2] today, he thought. It would be wonderful to do this with a radio.

Think of what you are doing.

You must do nothing stupid[3].

Then he said aloud, "I wish I had the boy To help me and to see this."

No one should be alone in their old age[4], he thought. But it is unavoidable[5]. I must remember to eat the tuna before he spoils[6] in order to keep strong. Remember, you must eat him in the morning, he said to himself.

1. come out 結果；演變
2. league [liːg] (n.) 聯盟
3. stupid [ˋstuːpɪd] (a.) 愚蠢的
4. in one's old age
   在一個人的老年
5. unavoidable [ˌʌnəˋvɔɪdəbl]
   (a.) 不可避免的
6. spoil [spɔɪl] (v.) 腐壞

7. porpoise [ˋpɔːrpəs]
   (n.) 海豚
8. come around 來到附近
9. blow [bloʊ] (v.) 噴水
   (blow-blew-blown)
10. make a joke 開玩笑
11. one another 彼此

During the night two porpoise[7] came around[8] the boat and he could hear them rolling and blowing[9].

"They are good," he said. "They play and make jokes[10] and love one another[11]. They are our brothers like the flying fish."

Then he began to pity[1] the great fish that he had hooked[2]. He is wonderful and strange and who knows how old he is, he thought. Never have I had such a strong fish nor one who acted so strangely. Perhaps he is too wise to jump. He could ruin[3] me by jumping. But what a great fish he is and what he will bring in the market if the flesh[4] is good. He took the bait like a male and he pulls like a male[5] and his fight has no panic[6] in it. I wonder if he has any plans or if he is just as desperate[7] as I am.

---

1. pity [ˈpɪti] (v.) 同情；憐憫
2. hook [hʊk] (v.) 鉤住
3. ruin [ˈruːɪn] (v.) 毀滅
4. flesh [fleʃ] (n.) 肉
5. male [meɪl] (n.) 男性
6. panic [ˈpænɪk] (n.) 驚慌
7. desperate [ˈdespərət] (a.) 絕望
8. settle [ˈsetl] (v.) 坐下
9. join [dʒɔɪn] (v.) 連結；作伴
10. surge [sɜːrdʒ] (n.) 大浪；波濤

"I wish the boy were here," he said aloud and settled[8] himself against the bow and felt the strength of the great fish through the line he held across his shoulders. My choice was to go out to find him beyond all people in the world. Now we are joined[9] together and no one to help either one of us.

The fish made a surge[10] that pulled him down[11] on his face and made a cut[12] below his eye. The blood ran down his cheek a little way. But it coagulated[13] and dried before it reached his chin[14] and he worked his way[15] back to the bow and rested against[16] the wood.

11. pull A down 把 A 往下拉
12. cut [kʌt] (n.) 割傷
13. coagulate [kouˋægjuleɪt] (v.) 凝結
14. chin [tʃɪn] (n.) 下巴
15. work one's way 努力前進
16. rest against 靠在……休息

I wonder why he made that surge, he thought. The wire must have slipped[1] on the great hill of his back. Certainly his back cannot feel as bad as mine does. But he cannot pull this skiff forever, no matter how[2] great he is.

"Fish," he said softly, aloud, "I'll stay with you until I am dead."

When the sun had risen further the old man realized that the fish was not getting tired[3]. There was only one favorable[4] sign. The slant of the line showed he was swimming at a lesser depth[5]. That did not mean that he would jump. But he might.

1. slip [slɪp] (v.) 滑動；滑落
2. no matter how 無論如何
3. get tired 變得疲倦
4. favorable [ˋfeɪvərəbl]
   (a.) 有利的
5. at a lesser depth
   在比較淺的深度
6. handle [ˋhændl]
   (v.) 應付；處理

56

"God, let him jump," the old man said. "I have enough line to handle[6] him."

"Fish," he said, "I love you and respect you very much. But I will kill you dead before this day ends."

A small bird came toward the skiff from the North. He was a warbler[7] and the old man could see he was very tired. He flew around the old man's head and rested on the line.

"How old are you?" the old man asked the bird. "Is this your first trip?" The bird was very tired and he teetered[8] on the line as his delicate feet gripped[9] it.

"Take a good rest[10], small bird," he said.

"Then go and take your chance[11] like any man or bird or fish."

---

7. warbler [ˋwɔːrblə(r)]
   (n.) 鳴禽
8. teeter [ˋtiːtə(r)] (v.)
   蹣跚；站不穩
9. grip [grɪp] (v.) 夾住；緊握
10. take a rest 休息
11. take chance 抓住機會

Just then the fish gave a sudden lurch[1] that pulled the old man down to the bow and would have pulled him overboard[2] if he had not braced himself and given some line.

The bird flew away[3] and he felt the line carefully with his right hand and noticed his hand was bleeding[4]. Shifting[5] the weight of the line to his left shoulder and kneeling carefully he washed his hand in the ocean.
The cut was in the working part of his hand. He knew he would need his hands before this was over[6] and he did not like to be cut before it started.

"Now," he said, "I must eat the small tuna."
He knelt down[7] and found the tuna under the stern. He put one knee on the fish and cut strips[8] of dark red meat from the back of the head to the tail.

1. lurch [lɜːrtʃ] (n.)
   突然搖晃；傾斜
2. overboard [ˈouvərbɔːrd]
   (adv.) 船外；落水
3. fly away 飛走
4. bleed [bliːd] (v.) 流血
   (bleed-bled-bled)
5. shift [ʃɪft] (v.) 移轉
6. over [ˈouvə(r)] (a.) 結束的
7. kneel down 跪下
8. strip [strɪp] (n.) 一片；一條
9. cramped [kræmpt] (a.) 抽筋
10. claw [klɔː] (n.) 爪子
11. do no good 沒有好處

"I don't think I can eat an entire one," he said.
He could feel the steady hard pull of the line
and his left hand was cramped[9].

"What kind of a hand is that," he said. "Cramp
then if you want. Make yourself into a claw[10].
It will do you no good[11]."

He picked up[12] a piece of tuna and put it in his
mouth and chewed[13] it slowly. It was not
unpleasant[14].
"How do you feel, hand?" he asked the cramped
hand that was almost as stiff[15] as rigor mortis[16].
"I'll eat some more for you."

I wish I could feed the fish, he thought. He is my
brother. But I must kill him and keep strong to
do it. Slowly he ate all the strips of fish.
"God help me to have the cramp go," he said.
"Because I do not know what the fish is going to
do." What is his plan, he thought. And what is
mine?

12. pick up 拿起
13. chew [tʃuː] (v.) 咀嚼
14. unpleasant [ʌnˋplɛznt] (a.)
     令人不愉快的
15. stiff [stɪf] (a.) 僵硬的
16. rigor mortis
     〔醫〕死後僵硬

His left hand was still cramped,

but he was unknotting[1] it slowly.

I hate cramps, he thought. It is a treachery[2] of one's own body. Then, with his right hand he felt the difference in the pull of the line.

"He's coming up," he said. "Come on hand. Please come on."

The line rose slowly and steadily and then the surface of the ocean bulged[3] ahead of the boat and the fish came out. He came out unendingly[4] and water poured[5] from his sides. He was bright in the sun and his head and his sides were wide and colored a light lavender[6]. His sword[7] was as long as a baseball bat and tapered[8] like a rapier[9] and he rose his full length[10] from the water and then re-entered it, smoothly, like a diver and the old man saw the great scythe-blade[11] of his tail go under[12], and the line started to race out[13].

1. unknot [ʌnˋnɑːt] (v.) 解開
2. treachery [ˋtretʃəri] (n.) 背叛；不忠
3. bulge [bʌldʒ] (v.) 膨脹；突起
4. unendingly [ʌnˋendŋli] (adv.) 無盡地；無終止地
5. pour [pɔː(r)] (v.) 傾注；傾瀉
6. light lavender 淡紫羅蘭色
7. sword [sɔːrd] (n.) 武器；劍
8. taper [ˋteɪpə(r)] (v.) （物體的一端）逐漸變尖細

"He is two feet longer than the skiff," the old man said. He was trying with both hands to keep the line just inside of breaking strength. He knew that if he could not slow the fish with a steady pressure, the fish could take out[14] all the line and break it.

9. rapier [ˋreɪpɪə(r)]
   (n.) 細長輕巧的劍
10. full length 全長
11. scythe-blade
    鐮刀般的魚鰭

12. go under 往下
13. race out 全速被拉走
14. take out 帶走

He is a great fish but I must convince[1] him that he is no match[2] for me, he thought.

I must never let him learn his strength nor what he could do if he made his run[3].

The old man had seen many great fish. He had seen many that weighed more than a thousand pounds and he had caught two of that size in his life, but never alone.

Now alone, and out of sight of[4] land, he was tied fast[5] to the biggest fish that he had ever seen and bigger than he had ever heard of, and his left hand was still cramped.

1. convince [kən`vɪns]
   (v.) 說服
2. match [mætʃ] (n.)
   對手；敵手
3. make one's run 開始跑
4. out of the sight of
   在視線外
5. fast [fæst] (adv.)
   緊緊地；牢固地
6. suffering [`sʌfə(r)ɪŋ]
   (a.) 受苦的
7. not . . . at all 完全不……
8. religious [rɪ`lɪdʒəs]
   (a.) 有宗教信仰的
9. pilgrimage [`pɪlgrɪmɪdʒ]
   (n.) 朝聖

I wonder why he jumped, the old man thought.
He jumped almost as though to show me how
big he was. I wish I could show him what sort
of man I am. But then he would see the
cramped hand.

At noon the old man's left hand was
uncramped. He was comfortable but suffering[6],
although he did not admit the suffering at all[7].

"I am not religious[8]," he said. "But I will say ten
Our Fathers and ten Hail Marys so that I can
catch this fish, and I promise to make a
pilgrimage[9] to the Virgin de Cobre if I catch him.
Christ, I did not know he was so big."

"I'll kill him though," he said. "In all his greatness."
Although it is unjust[1], he thought.
But I will show him what a man can do and what a man endures[2].

"I told the boy I was a strange old man," he said.
"Now is when I must prove[3] it."
The thousand times that he had proved it meant nothing. Now he was proving it again.
"If you're not tired, fish," he said aloud, "you must be very strange."

He felt very tired now and he tried to think of other things. He thought of the Big Leagues[4], and he knew the Yankees of New York were playing the Tigers of Detroit.

1. unjust [ˌʌnˋdʒʌst]
   (a.) 不公平的
2. endure [ɪnˋdʊr]
   (v.) 忍受;忍耐
3. prove [pruːv] (v.) 證明
4. Big League 大聯盟
5. have confidence 有信心
6. be worthy of
   值得;配的上的
7. I am sure (that) . . .
   我肯定……

64

This is the second day that I do not know the
result of the *juegos,* he thought. But I must have
confidence[5] and I must be worthy of[6] the great
DiMaggio who does all things perfectly.

Do you believe the great DiMaggio would stay
with a fish as long as I will stay with this one?
he thought. I am sure[7] he would and more since
he is young and strong. Also his father was a
fisherman.

Man and Nature

As far back as ancient cave paintings, art has been strongly influenced by Nature. Ever since humans became aware of Nature, they have sometimes thought of Her as a competitor or as a provider. Throughout human history, natural forces have caused great hardship and loss of life. On both land and sea, humankind has had to battle nature to survive. This struggle is represented in different types of art throughout the centuries.

For example, Beethoven's sixth symphony expresses the violence of a thunderstorm. Herman Melville's novel "Moby Dick" is a masterpiece in literature that depicts the struggle between a man and Nature. Hemingway's "The Old Man and the Sea" is another example of this theme.

However, Hemingway's old man is not always fighting Nature. Nature provides the old man with food. Even a lost bird provides the old man with some company in his lonely battle. The old man does not regard Nature as his enemy. Instead he thinks of the sea as a woman who changes her mood frequently. Sometimes she is kind and loving, but sometimes she is cruel and unforgiving.

CHAPTER FOUR

An Even¹ Fight

As the sun set, to give himself more confidence, he remembered the time in the tavern at Casablanca when he had played the hand game² with the great negro³ from Cienfuegos, who was the strongest man on the docks⁴.

They had gone one day and one night with their elbows⁵ on a chalk⁶ line on the table. Each one was trying to force the other's hand down onto the table. They changed the referee every four hours so that the referees⁷ could sleep.

1. **even** [ˋɪːvn] (a.)
   對等的；相等的
2. **play the hand game**
   比腕力
3. **negro** [ˋniːɡroʊ] (n.) 黑人
4. **dock** [dɑːk] (n.) 碼頭
5. **elbow** [ˋelboʊ] (n.) 手肘
6. **chalk** [tʃɔːk] (n.) 粉筆
7. **referee** [ˌrefəˋriː] (n.) 裁判
8. **odds** [ɑːdz] (n.) 機率
9. **back and forth** 來來回回
10. **El Campeon** 冠軍
11. **off balance** 失去平衡
12. **athlete** [ˋæθliːt] (n.) 運動員
13. **beaten** [biːtn] (a.) 被打敗的
14. **at daylight** 白晝

The odds[8] would change back and forth[9] all
night. Once the negro had the old man, who
was not an old man then but was Santiago El
Campeon[10], nearly three inches off balance[11].

But the old man had raised his hand again.
He was sure then that he had the negro, who
was a fine man and a great athlete[12], beaten[13].
And at daylight[14] he had forced the hand of the
negro down and down until it rested on the
table. The match had started on a Sunday
morning and ended on a Monday morning.

For a long time everyone had called him 'The Champion.' After that he had a few matches[1] and then no more. He decided that he could beat[2] anyone if he wanted to badly[3] enough and he decided that it was bad for his right hand for fishing.

1. match [mætʃ] (n.)
   比賽；競爭
2. beat [biːt] (v.) 打敗
   (beat-beat-beaten)
3. badly [ˋbædli] (adv.)
   非常；很
4. weed [wiːd] (n.) 野草
5. jump in the air 在空中跳躍

Just before it was dark, as they passed a great island of Sargasso weed[4], his small line was taken by a dolphin. He saw it first when it jumped in the air[5], bending and flapping[6] wildly. When it was at the stern the old man leaned over[7] and lifted the burnished[8] gold fish with its purple spots[9] over the stern.

Its jaws[10] were working convulsively[11] in quick bites against the hook. It pounded[12] the bottom of the skiff with its long flat body, its tail and its head until he clubbed it. Then it shivered[13] and was still[14].

The old man watched the sun go into the ocean and the slant[15] of the big cord.

"He hasn't changed at all," he said.

But watching the movement of the water against his hand he noted[16] that it was a bit slower.

---

6. flap [flæp] (v.) 拍打；拍動
7. lean over 傾身；曲身
8. burnished [ˈbɜːrnɪʃt] (a.) 光滑的
9. spot [spɑːt] (n.) 斑點
10. jaw [dʒɔː] (n.) 上下顎
11. convulsively [kənˈvʌlsɪvli] (adv.) 騷動地；震動地
12. pound [paʊnd] (v.) 猛擊
13. shiver [ˈʃɪvə(r)] (v.) 顫抖
14. still [stɪl] (a.) 靜止的；不動的
15. slant [slænt] (v.) 傾斜
16. note [noʊt] (v.) 注意；留意

"I'll lash[1] the two oars together across the stern and that will slow him in the night," he said. "He's good[2] for the night and so am I."

I'm learning how to do it, he thought. This part of it anyway. Then, too, remember he hasn't eaten since he took the bait[3] and he is huge and needs much food. I have eaten the whole bonito[4]. Tomorrow I will eat the dolphin.

1. lash [læʃ] (v.)
   以繩索綁起來
2. be good 有利的；有益的
3. take the bait 吞下誘餌
4. bonito 鰹魚
5. How do you feel?
   你覺得如何？
6. dullness [dʌlnəs]
   (n.) 麻木；無感覺
7. be gone 消失

"How do you feel[5], fish?" he asked aloud. "I feel good and my left hand is better and I have food for a night and a day. Pull the boat, fish."

He did not truly feel good because the pain from the cord across his back had almost passed pain and gone into a dullness[6] that worried him.

But I have had worse things than that, he thought. My hand is only cut a little and the cramp is gone[7] from the other.
My legs are all right.

It was dark now as it becomes dark quickly after the sun sets in September. The first stars were out[8]. He did not know the name of Rigel[9] but he saw it and knew that soon they would all be out and he would have all his distant[10] friends.

8. be out 消逝；不見
9. Rigel 〔天〕獵戶星座的
　　　其中一顆星
10. distant ['dɪstənt] (a.) 遠方的

"The fish is my friend too," he said aloud.
"I have never seen or heard of such a fish.
But I must kill him. I am glad we do not have to
try to kill the stars."
Then he was sorry for the great fish that had
nothing to eat and his determination[1] to kill him
never relaxed[2] in his sorrow[3] for him.
How many people will he feed, he thought.
But are they worthy to eat him? No, of course
not. There is no one worthy of[4] eating a fish
with such great dignity[5].

The old man rested for what he believed to be
two hours. The moon did not rise until late now
and he had no way of[6] judging the time.
He was still bearing[7] the pull of the fish across
his shoulders.
"But you have not slept yet, old man. It is half a
day and a night and now another day and you
have not slept," he said aloud. "I must devise[8] a
way so that you sleep a little if he is quiet and
steady. If you do not sleep you might become
unclear in the head."

1. determination
   [dɪˌtɜːrmɪneɪʃn] (n.) 決心
2. relax [rɪˋlæks] (v.)
   鬆懈；放寬
3. sorrow [ˋsɔːroʊ]
   (n.) 遺憾；悲傷
4. worthy of 應得；值得

I could go without[9] sleeping, he told himself. But it would be too dangerous.

He worked his way back to the stern. The stars were bright now and he saw the dolphin clearly and he pushed the blade of his knife into his head and pulled him out from under the stern.

The dolphin was cold and gray-white now in the starlight[10] and the old man skinned[11] one side of him while he held his right foot on the fish's head. Then he skinned the other side and cut fillets[12]. He leaned over the side and put his hand in the water. The flow[13] of the water against it was less strong.

"He is tired or he is resting. Now let me eat this dolphin and get some rest[14] and a little sleep."

5. dignity [ˋdɪgnəti] (n.)
   尊嚴；尊嚴
6. have no way of . . .
   沒有辦法……
7. bear [ber] (v.) 忍受
8. devise [dɪˋvaɪz]
   (v.) 想出；策畫

9. without [wɪˋðaut]
   (prep.) 無；沒有
10. in the starlight 在星光下
11. skin [skɪn] (v.) 剝皮
12. fillet [fɪˋleɪ] (n.) 魚片
13. flow [floʊ] (n.) 流動
14. get some rest 休息一下

Under the stars he ate half of one of the dolphin fillets.

"What an excellent fish dolphin is to eat cooked[1]," he said. "And what a miserable[2] fish raw[3]. I will never go in a boat again without salt or limes[4]."

1. cooked [kʊkt] (a.) 煮熟的
2. miserable [ˈmɪzrəbl] (a.) 令人難受的
3. raw [rɔ:] (a.) 生的；未煮過的
4. lime [laɪm] (n.) 萊姆
5. cloud [klaʊd] (v.) 遮蔽；覆蓋
6. one after another 一個接一個
7. canyon [ˈkanjən] (n.) 峽谷
8. drop [drɑ:p] (v.) 停止

The sky was clouding[5] over to the East and one
after another[6] the stars he knew were gone.
It looked now as though he were moving into a
great canyon[7] of clouds and the wind had
dropped[8].

"There will be bad weather in three or four
days," he said. "But not tonight or tomorrow.
Rig[9] now to get some sleep, old man,
while the fish is calm and steady."

The moon had been up for a long time[10] but he
slept on and the fish pulled on steadily[11] and the
boat moved into the tunnel of clouds. He woke
with the jerk[12] of his right fist coming up
against his face and the line burning out[13]
through his right hand. He could not feel the
line with his left hand but he braked[14] all he
could with his right and the line rushed out.

9. rig [rɪg] (v.)
   裝置（船上）設備
10. for a long time
    很長一段時間
11. steadily [ˈstedəli]
    (adv.) 平穩地

12. jerk [dʒɜːrk] (n.) 猛然一動
13. burn out 發熱
14. brake [breɪk] (v.) 煞住

Finally his left hand found the line and he leaned back[1] against it and now it burned his back and his left hand. His left hand was taking all the strain[2] and it was cutting badly.

Just then the fish jumped making a great bursting of the ocean and then a heavy fall. Then he jumped again and again and the boat was going fast although line was still racing out[3] and the old man was raising the strain to the breaking point[4]. He had been pulled down tight on to the bow and his face was in the cut slice of dolphin and he could not move.

This is what we waited for, he thought.
So now let us take it.
Make him pay for[5] the line. Make him pay for it.

1. lean back 往後靠
2. strain [streɪn]
   (n.) 張力；負擔
3. race out 急速減少
4. to the breaking point
   幾乎被扯斷
5. pay for . . .
   為⋯⋯付出代價

6. splash [splæʃ] (n.) 濺水聲
7. get one's head up
   把頭抬高
8. be on one's knees 跪下
9. rise to one's feet 站起身

78

He could not see the fish's jumps but only heard the breaking of the ocean and the heavy splash[6] as he fell. The speed of the line was cutting his hands badly but he had always known this would happen.

If the boy were here he would wet the coils of line, he thought. Yes. If the boy were here.

The line went out but it was slowing now and he was making the fish earn each inch of it. Now he got his head up[7] from the wood and out of the slice of fish that his cheek had crushed. He was on his knees[8] and then he rose to his feet[9]. He was giving line but more slowly all the time.

I wonder what started him so suddenly?
Could it have been hunger that made him
desperate, or was he frightened[1] by something
in the night?
Maybe he suddenly felt fear. But he was such a
calm, strong fish and he seemed so fearless and
so confident. It is strange.
"You better be fearless and confident yourself,
old man," he said.

The old man held him with his left hand and
stooped down[2] and scooped up[3] water in his
right hand to get the crushed dolphin flesh off
his face[4]. He was afraid that it might nauseate[5]
him and cause him to vomit[6] and lose his
strength[7]. He washed his right hand in the
water and then let it stay in the salt water while
he watched the first light come before the
sunrise. He's headed almost East, he thought.
That means he is tired and going with the
current. Soon he will have to circle.
Then our true work begins.

1. be frightened 害怕；驚嚇
2. stoop down 曲身；彎腰
3. scoop up 舀起
4. get A off one's face
   把臉上的 A 撥掉
5. nauseate [ˈnɔːsieɪt]
   (v.) 感到噁心
6. vomit [ˈvɑːmɪt] (v.) 嘔吐
7. lose one's strength
   喪失力量 (lose-lost-lost)

After he judged that his right hand had been in the water long enough he took it out and looked at it.

"It is not bad," he said. "And pain does not matter[8] to a man."

He took hold of[9] the line carefully so that it did not fit into any of the fresh line cuts and shifted[10] his weight so that he could put his left hand into the sea on the other side of the skiff.

8. matter [ˈmætə(r)]
   (v.) 要緊；重要
9. take hold of 握住
10. shift [ʃɪft] (v.) 移轉

"You did not do so badly for something worthless[1]," he said to his left hand. "But there was a moment when I could not find you."

Why was I not born with[2] two good hands? he thought. Perhaps it was my fault in not training the left one properly. But God knows he had enough chances to learn. He did not do so badly in the night, though, and he has cramped only once. If he cramps again let the line cut him off. The sun was rising for the third time since he had set out[3] to sea when the fish started to circle[4].

"It is a very big circle," he said.

"But he is circling."

I must hold all I can, he thought. The strain will shorten his circle each time. Perhaps in an hour[5] I will see him. Now I must convince him and then I must kill him.

1. worthless [ˋwɑːrθləs]
   (a.) 無價值的
2. be born with 與生俱來
3. set out 啓程
4. circle [ˋsɜːrkl] (v.) 繞圈
5. in an hour 一小時後
6. be wet with sweat
   因流汗而濕透
7. be tired deep into one's
   bones 極爲疲累
8. salt [sɔːlt] (v.) 撒鹽
9. feel faint and dizzy
   覺得暈眩

But the fish kept on circling slowly and the old man was wet with sweat[6] and tired deep into his bones[7] two hours later. But the circles were much shorter now and from the way the line slanted he could tell the fish had risen steadily while he swam.

For an hour the old man had been seeing black spots before his eyes and the sweat salted[8] his eyes and salted the cut under his eye and on his forehead. He was not afraid of the black spots. Twice, though, he had felt faint and dizzy[9] and that had worried him.

"I cannot fail and die on a fish like this," he said. "Now that[1] I have him coming so beautifully. God help me endure[2]. I'll say a hundred Our Fathers and a hundred Hail Marys. But I cannot say them now."

Consider[3] them said, he thought. I'll say them later.

Just then he felt a sudden banging[4] and jerking on the line he held with his two hands. It was sharp and heavy.

He is hitting the wire with his sword, he thought. He may jump and I would rather[5] he circled now. The jumps were necessary for him to take air[6]. But after that each jump can widen[7] the opening[8] of the hook wound[9] and he can throw the hook.

1. now that 既然
2. endure [ɪnˋdʊr]
   (v.) 忍受；忍耐
3. consider [kənˋsɪdə(r)]
   (v.) 認為
4. banging [ˋbæŋɪŋ]
   (n.) 重擊聲
5. would rather 寧願
6. take air 獲得空氣
7. widen [ˋwaɪdn] (v.) 使變寬
8. opening [ˋoʊpnɪŋ]
   (n.) 縫隙；開口
9. wound [wuːnd] (n.) 傷口
10. give up 放棄

"Don't jump, fish," he said.
"Don't jump."
The fish hit the wire several
times more, and each time the
old man gave up[10] a little line.

After a while[11] the fish stopped beating at the
wire and started circling slowly again. The old
man was gaining line steadily now. But he felt
faint again. He lifted some sea water with his
left hand and put it on his head. Then he put
more on and rubbed[12] the back of his neck.
"I have no cramps," he said. "He'll be up soon
and I can last[13]. You have to last. Don't even
speak of it."

He kneeled against the bow and, for a moment[14],
slipped the line over his back again. I'll rest now
while he circles and then stand up and work on
him when he comes in, he decided.

11. after a while
　　過了一段時間
12. rub [rʌb] (v.) 揉；摩擦

13. last [læst] (v.) 堅持
14. for a moment 有一瞬間

I'm more tired than I have ever been, he
thought, and now the trade wind[1] is rising.
But that will be good to take him in with.
The sea had risen considerably[2].
But it was a fair weather[3] breeze and he had to
have it to get home.
"I'll just steer[4] south and west," he said. "A man
is never lost[5] at sea and it is a long island."

It was on the third turn that he saw the fish for
the first time. He saw him first as a dark
shadow that took so long to pass under the boat
that he could not believe its length[6].
"No," he said. "He can't be[7] that big."
But he was that big and at the end of this circle
he came to the surface[8] only thirty yards away
and the man saw his tail out of the water.
It was higher than a big scythe blade and a very
pale lavender above the dark blue water.

1. trade wind 季節風
2. considerably
   [kən`sɪdərəbli] (adv.)
   頗爲；相當高地
3. fair weather 舒適的天氣
4. steer [stɪr] (v.) 改變方向
5. be lost 迷失；迷路

6. length [lɛŋθ] (n.) 長度
7. can't be . . .
   不可能會是……
8. come to the surface
   來到表面
9. bulk [bʌlk] (n.) 體積；大小
10. stripe [straɪp] (n.) 條紋

As the fish swam just below the surface the old man could see his huge bulk[9] and purple stripes[10]. His dorsal[11] fin[12] was down and his huge pectorals[13] were spread wide[14].
Then the old man could see the fish's eye.

The old man was sweating now but from something else besides[15] the sun. On each placid[16] turn the fish made he was gaining line and he was sure that in two turns he would have a chance to get the harpoon in.

11. dorsal [ˈdɔːrsl] (a.) 背部的
12. fin [fɪn] (n.) 鰭
13. pectoral [ˈpɛktərəl]
　　(a.) 胸部的
14. be spread wide
　　伸展得極寬
15. besides [bɪˈsaɪdz]
　　(prep.) 除……以外
16. placid [ˈplæsɪd]
　　(a.) 平靜的；溫和的

But I must get him close[1], close, close, he
thought. I mustn't try for[2] the head.
I must get the heart.
"Be calm and strong, old man," he said.

The fish was coming in on his circle now calm
and beautiful with only his great tail moving.
The old man pulled on him to bring him closer.
For just a moment the fish turned a little on his
side. Then he straightened[3] himself and began
another circle.
"I moved him," the old man said.
"I moved him then."

He felt faint again but he held on to the great
fish with all his strength[4]. I moved him, he
thought. Maybe this time I can get him over[5].
Pull, hands, he thought. Hold up[6], legs.
Last for me, head. Last for me. You never went.
This time I'll pull him over.

1. get A close 讓 A 靠近
2. try for 想辦法達到……
3. straighten [ˈstreɪtn]
   (v.) 變直
4. with all one's strength
   用盡力氣
5. over [ˈoʊvə(r)] (adv.) 終結
6. hold up 保持強壯
7. forth [fɔːrθ] (prep.)
   向前；往前方
8. right [raɪt] (v.) 修正

But when he put forth[7] all of his effort, the fish
righted[8] himself and swam away.

"Fish," the old man said. "Fish, you are going to
have to die anyway. Do you have to kill me too?"

That way nothing is accomplished[1], he thought. His mouth was too dry to speak but he could not reach for[2] the water now. I must get him alongside[3] this time, he thought. I am not good for many more turns. Yes, you are, he told himself. You're good forever.

On the next turn, he nearly had him. But again the fish righted himself and swam away slowly.

You are killing me, fish, the old man thought. But you have a right to. Never have I seen a greater, or more beautiful or a calmer or more noble[4] thing than you, brother. Come on and kill me. I do not care[5] who kills who. Now you are getting confused[6] in the head, he thought. You must keep your head clear and know how to suffer like a man or a fish.

1. accomplish [əˋkɑːmplɪʃ]
   (v.) 完成；達到
2. reach for 拿到
3. alongside [əˏlɔːŋˋsaɪd]
   (prep.) 在……旁邊；並排
4. noble [ˋnoʊbl] (a.) 高貴的
5. care [ker] (v.) 在乎
6. get confused 變得混亂
7. clear up 澄清
8. mushy [ˋmʌʃi] (a.) 柔軟的
9. flash [flæʃ] (n.) 閃光

"Clear up, head," he said in a voice he could hardly hear. "Clear up[7]."

He tried it once more and he felt himself going when he turned the fish. The fish righted himself and swam off again slowly with the great tail moving in the air.

I'll try it again, the old man promised, although his hands were mushy[8] now and he could only see well in flashes[9].

Comprehension Quiz

A True or False.

1 The old man does not respect the fish
he caught.
T F

2 His left hand has cramped only once.
T F

3 The old man's hero is Joe DiMaggio.
T F

4 The old man wanted the big fish to jump to
make his hook wound wide.
T F

5 By the time the old man had the fish close to
the boat, he was near the end of his strength.
T F

B Choose the correct answer.

1 Choose the sentence that best describes the old man.

(a) He's one to give up easily.

(b) He will fight to his last breath.

(c) He likes to have expensive and fancy things.

(d) He complains too much.

2 What happened to the old man's left hand?

(a) It became cramped.

(b) It was bleeding very much.

(c) He crushed it under the oar.

(d) It was cut off from the pressure of the fishing line.

C Fill in the blanks with the given words.

> poured lurch as long as strange fillets

1. He cut the dolphin up into _____.

2. Water _____ from the sides of the fish when it jumped.

3. The fish's sword was _____ a baseball bat.

4. The old man said to the boy, "I am a _____ old man."

5. The big fish surprised the old man with a powerful _____.

D Rearrange the sentences in chronological order.

1. The big fish jumped.

2. The old man got some sleep.

3. The old man ate some of the dolphin.

4. A small bird visited the old man.

5. The old man remembered that he had won a arm-wrestling contest.

_____ ⇨ _____ ⇨ _____ ⇨ _____ ⇨ _____

CHAPTER FIVE

Shark Attack

He took all his pain and what was left of his strength and his long-gone[1] pride and he put it against the fish's agony[2].

1. long-gone 消失已久的
2. agony [ˈægəni]
   (n.) 極大的痛苦
3. gently [ˈdʒɛntli]
   (adv.) 溫和地
4. chest fin 胸鰭
5. lean [liːn] (v.) 傾斜；倚靠
6. push all one's weight after
   用盡全力推向⋯⋯
7. width [wɪdθ] (n.) 寬度
8. crash [kræʃ]
   (n.) 巨大的衝擊聲

The fish came over onto his side and swam gently[3] and started to pass the boat.

The old man dropped the line and put his foot on it and lifted the harpoon as high as he could and drove it down with all his strength into the fish's side just behind the great chest fin[4].
He felt the iron go in and he leaned[5] on it and drove it further and then pushed all his weight after[6] it.

Then the fish came alive, with his death in him, and rose high out of the water showing all his great length and width[7] and all his power and his beauty. He seemed to hang in the air above the old man in the skiff. Then he fell into the water with a crash[8].

The old man felt faint[1] and sick and he could not see well. But he cleared[2] the harpoon line and let it run slowly through his raw[3] hands and, when he could see, he saw the fish was on his back with his silver belly[4] up.

The shaft[5] of the harpoon was projecting[6] at an angle[7] from the fish's shoulder and the sea was red with the blood from his heart. The fish was silvery[8] and still and floated[9] with the waves. The old man laid his head on his hands.

"Keep my head clear," he said. "I am a tired old man. But I have killed this fish which is my brother and now I must do the slave work[10]."

1. faint [feɪnt] (a.) 快要暈倒的
2. clear [klɪr] (v.)
   清理；使乾淨
3. raw [rɔ:] (a.)
   擦傷的；刺痛的
4. belly [`bɛli] (n.) 腹部
5. shaft [ʃæft] (n.) 箭尖
6. project [`prɑ:dʒɛkt]
   (v.) 投擲
7. at an angle 從一種角度

Now I must prepare the rope to tie him
alongside the skiff, he thought.
This skiff will never hold[11] him.

He started to pull the fish in[12] to have him
alongside the skiff. I want to see him,
he thought, and to touch and to feel him.
He is my fortune[13], he thought. But that is not
why I wish to feel him. I think I felt his heart
when I pushed on the harpoon the second time.
Bring him in now and get the noose[14] around his
tail and another around his middle to tie him to
the skiff.

8. silvery [ˋsɪlvəri] (a.) 銀色的
9. float [floʊt] (v.) 漂浮
10. slave work 苦工
11. hold [hoʊld] (v.) 支撐住

12. pull A in 把 A 拖進……
13. fortune [ˋfɔːrtʃuːn] (n.) 財產
14. noose [nuːs] (n.) 繩索

"Get to work, old man," he said. He took a very small drink of[1] water.

"There is much slave work to do now that the fight is over[2]."

He looked up at[3] the sky and then out to his fish.

"Come on, fish," he said. But the fish did not come. Instead he lay[4] there and the old man pulled the skiff up to him.

When the fish's head was against the bow[5] he could not believe his size.

"It was the only way to kill him," the old man said. He was feeling better and his head was clear. He's over fifteen hundred pounds, he thought. Maybe much more.

"I think the great DiMaggio would be proud of me today."

1. take a drink of . . .
   喝一口……
2. over [ˈouvə(r)] (a.) 結束的
3. look up at 往上看……
4. lie [laɪ] (v.) 躺；橫臥
   (lie-lay-lain)
5. bow [baʊ] (n.) 船頭
6. fasten to 綁在……
7. stern [stɜːrn] (n.) 船尾
8. thwart [θwɔːrt]
   (n.) 船上的座板
9. lash [læʃ] (v.) 用繩索綁

He fastened[6] the fish to the bow, to the stern[7]
and to the middle thwart[8]. He was so big it was
like lashing[9] a much bigger skiff alongside.

He could see the fish and he had only to look at
his hands and feel his back against the stern to
know that this had truly happened and was not
a dream.

They were sailing together lashed side by side[1] and the old man thought, let him bring me in if it pleases[2] him. I am only better than him through trickery[3] and he meant[4] me no harm.

It was an hour before the first shark hit him. The shark had come up[5] from deep down in the water as the dark cloud of blood had settled[6] and dispersed[7] in the mile-deep sea.

He had come up so fast that he broke[8] the surface of the blue water and was in the sun. Then he fell back into the sea and picked up[9] the scent[10] and started following the skiff and the fish.

1. side by side 並排；一起
2. please [pliːz] (v.)
   使愉悅；使高興
3. trickery [ˋtrɪkəri]
   (n.) 詭計；取巧
4. mean [miːn]
   (v.) 存心；意圖
5. come up 游上來
6. settle [ˋsetl] (v.) 下降
7. disperse [dɪˋspɜːrs]
   (v.) 散開
8. break [breɪk] (v.)
   打破；破碎
9. pick up 找到
10. scent [sent] (n.)
    氣味；味道

Sometimes he lost the scent. But he would pick it up again and he swam fast and hard. He was a very big Mako shark built[1] to swim as fast as the fastest fish in the sea and everything about him was beautiful except his jaws[2].

His back was as blue as a swordfish's[3] and his belly was silver and his hide[4] was smooth[5] and handsome. Inside the closed double lip of his jaws all of his eight rows[6] of teeth were slanted[7] inwards[8]. They were not the ordinary pyramid-shaped[9] teeth of most sharks.
They were shaped like a man's fingers when they are curled[10] like claws[11].
They were nearly as long as the fingers of the old man and they had razor-sharp[12] cutting edges[13] on both sides.

1. built [bɪlt] (a.)
   有……構造的
2. jaw [dɔ:] (n.) 顎
3. swordfish [ˈsɔːrdfɪʃ]
   (n.) 旗魚
4. hide [haɪd] (n.) 皮
5. smooth [smuːθ] (a.) 光滑的

6. row [roʊ] (n.) 一排；一列
7. be slanted 傾斜
8. inwards [ˈɪnwərdz]
   (adv.) 向內地
9. pyramid-shaped
   金字塔型的
10. curled [kɜːrld] (a.) 捲曲的

When the old man saw him coming he knew that this was a shark that had no fear at all and would do exactly what he wished.
He prepared the harpoon and the rope while he watched the shark come forward.

The old man's head was clear and good now and he was full of resolution[14] but he had little hope.
It was too good to last, he thought.
It might as well[15] have been a dream.
I cannot keep him from hitting me but maybe I can get him. *Dentuso,* he thought. Bad luck to your mother.

---

11. claw [klɔ:] (n.) 爪子
12. razor-sharp
    像剃刀一樣銳利
13. cutting edges 切口

14. resolution [ˌrezəˈluːʃn]
    (n.) 決心
15. might as well 也同樣可能

When the shark hit the fish the old man saw his mouth open and his strange eyes. He heard the clicking[1] sound of the teeth as he tore[2] into the meat just above the tail. He rammed[3] the harpoon down into the shark's head and into his brain. He hit it with his bloody hands driving the harpoon with all his strength. He hit it without hope but with resolution and complete malignancy[4].

The shark swung[5] over and the old man saw his eye was not alive. The old man knew that he was dead but the shark would not accept it. It ploughed[6] over the water as a speed-boat[7] does. Then he lay quietly for a little while and went down very slowly.

"He took about forty pounds and my harpoon," the old man said. He did not like to look at the fish any more since he had been mutilated[8]. When the fish had been hit it was as though[9] he himself were hit.

1. clicking [klɪkɪŋ] (n.) 喀嚓聲
2. tear [ter] (v.) 撕扯；撕裂
   (tear-tore-torn)
3. ram [ræm] (v.) 猛撞；推擠
4. malignancy [mə`lɪgnənsi]
   (n.) 敵意；惡意
5. swing [swɪŋ] (v.)
   搖擺；擺動
   (swing-swung-swung)
6. plough [plaʊ] (v.) 破浪前進
7. speed boat 汽艇

It was too good to last, he thought. I wish it had been a dream now and that I had never hooked[10] the fish and was alone in bed on the newspapers.

"But man is not made for defeat," he said. "A man can be destroyed but not defeated[11]." I am sorry that I killed the fish though, he thought. Now the bad time is coming and I do not even have the harpoon.
"Don't think, old man," he said aloud. "Sail on and take it when it comes."

8. mutilate [ˋmjuːtɪleɪt]
     (v.) 毀壞；殘缺不全
9. as though 如同；彷彿
10. hook [hʊk] (v.) 釣上
11. be defeated 被擊敗

He knew quite well the pattern[1] of what could happen when he reached the inner part of the current[2]. But there was nothing to be done now.

"Yes, there is," he said aloud[3]. "I can lash my knife to the butt[4] of one of the oars."
So he did that.
"Now, I am still an old man. But I am not unarmed[5]."
He watched only the forward part of the fish and some of his hope returned.

It is silly not to hope, he thought. Besides I believe it is a sin. Do not think about sin[6]. There are enough problems now without sin. I have no understanding of[7] it and I am not sure that I believe in it. Perhaps it was a sin to kill the fish. I suppose it was though I did it to keep me alive and feed many people. But then everything is a sin. Do not think about sin. You were born to[8] be a fisherman.

---

1. pattern [ˈpætərn]
   (n.) 模式；樣式
2. current [ˈkɜːrənt]
   (n.) 洋流；海流
3. aloud [əˈlaʊd] (adv.)
   大聲地；響亮地

4. butt [bʌt] (n.) 較粗的一端
5. unarmed [ʌnˈɑːrmd]
   (a.) 徒手的；無武器的
6. sin [sɪn] (n.) 罪惡；罪孽
7. have no understanding
   of ... 對……不了解

You did not kill the fish only to keep alive and to sell for food, he thought. You killed him for pride and because you are a fisherman.
You loved him when he was alive and you loved him after. If you love him it is not a sin to kill him. Or is it more?

But you enjoyed killing the *dentuso*, he thought. "I killed him in self-defense[9]," the old man said aloud. "And I killed him well."
Besides, he thought, everything kills everything else in some way. Fishing kills me exactly as it keeps me alive. The boy keeps me alive.
I must not deceive[10] myself too much.

8. be born to . . . 天生的
9. self-defense 自衛
10. deceive [dɪ`si:v] (v.) 欺騙

The Caribbean Sea

The three largest of the major seas are, in order of size, South China, Mediterranean and Caribbean. The South China Sea is commonly featured in today's headlines as China, Vietnam, Malaysia and the Philippines and each try to control the resources found there. The Mediterranean was very important in the development of early Western civilization. Finally, the Caribbean is famous for its clear waters, beautiful coral and abundant marine life. It is also famous as the setting for Hemingway's "The Old Man and the Sea."

The Caribbean is a favorite destination for tourists who enjoy fishing, scuba diving, relaxing on white beaches or swimming in clear blue waters. Many islands that used to be colonies of European nations are located there. Cuba is the largest of these islands, and is unique as one of the last surviving socialist nations. The capital of Cuba, Havana, is featured in Hemingway's story. This capital used to be a famous tourist destination for rich and famous Americans, but since socialist government took power, Havana lost its appeal as a tourist destination.

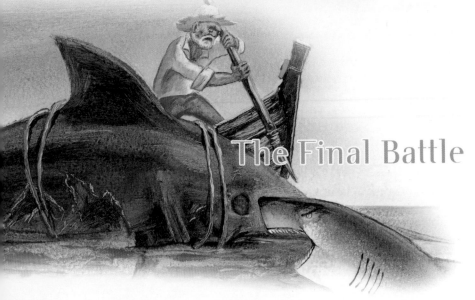

The Final Battle

He had been sailing for two hours when he saw the first of the two sharks.

"*Galanos*," he said aloud.

He took up the oar with the knife lashed to it. He lifted it as lightly as he could because his hands rebelled at[1] the pain, and he watched the sharks come.

1. rebel at . . . 對……反感
2. scavenger [ˈskævɪndʒə(r)] (n.) 以腐屍爲食的動物
3. rudder [ˈrʌdə(r)] (n.) 船舵
4. go out of the sight 失去蹤影
5. jerk [dʒɜːrk] (v.) 猛推
6. spinal cord 脊髓
7. withdraw [wɪθˈdrɔː] (v.) 抽回 (withdraw-withdrew-withdrawn)

They were hateful sharks, bad-smelling scavengers[2] as well as killers, and when they were hungry they would bite at an oar or the rudder[3] of a boat.

"*Ay*," the old man said. "*Galanos*. Come on, *Galanos*."

They came. One turned and went out of sight[4] under the skiff and the old man could feel the skiff shake as he jerked[5] and pulled on the fish. The other watched the old man with his yellow eyes and then came in fast to hit the fish where he had already been bitten.

A line showed clearly on the top of his brown head and back where the brain joined the spinal cord[6] and the old man drove the knife on the oar into the brain, withdrew[7] it, and drove it in again into the shark's yellow cat-like eyes. The shark let go of the fish and slid[8] down, swallowing[9] what he had taken as he died.

8. slide [slaɪd] (v.) 滑動
   (slide-slid-slid)
9. swallow [ˋswɑːloʊ] (v.) 吞下

When he saw the other shark he leaned over the side and punched him. The blow[1] hurt his hands and his shoulder. But the shark came up fast with his head out and the old man hit him squarely[2] in the center of his flat-topped[3] head. The old man withdrew the blade[4] and punched the shark exactly in the same spot[5] again. The old man stabbed[6] him in his left eye but the shark still hung[7] there.

1. blow [bloʊ] (n.) 一擊
2. squarely [ˋskwerli] (adv.) 筆直地
3. flat-topped 頂部平坦的
4. blade [bleɪd] (n.) 刀；刃
5. spot [spɑːt] (n.) 部位；位置
6. stab [stæb] (v.) 刺
7. hang [hæŋ] (v.) 逗留；徘徊 (hang-hung-hung)

"No?" the old man said and he drove the blade between the vertebrae[8] and the brain and he felt the cartilage[9] break.

"Go on, *galano*. Slide down a mile deep. Go and see your friend, or maybe it's your mother." The old man wiped[10] the blade of his knife and laid down[11] the oar. Then he brought the skiff on to her course.

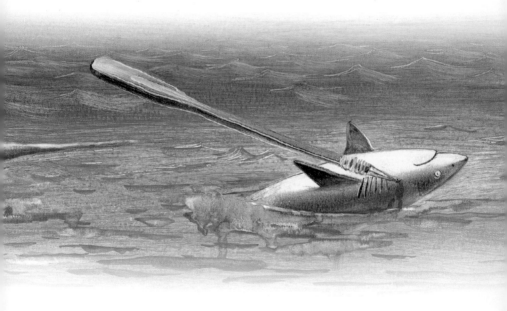

8. vertebrae [ˋvɑːrtɪbrə]
    (n.) 脊椎骨（複數）
9. cartilage [ˋkɑːrtɪlɪdʒ]
    (n.) 軟骨

10. wipe [waɪp] (v.) 擦淨
11. lay down 放下

"They must have taken a quarter of[1] him and of the best meat," he said aloud. "I wish it were a dream and that I had never hooked him. I'm sorry about it, fish. It makes everything wrong." He stopped and he did not want to look at the fish now.

"I shouldn't have gone out so far, fish," he said. "Neither for you nor for me. I'm sorry, fish. God knows how much that last one took," he continued. "But she's much lighter now." He did not want to think of the mutilated underside of the fish.

He was a fish to keep a man all winter, he thought. Don't think of that. Just rest and try to get your hands in shape[2] to defend what is left of him. The next shark that came was a single shovel-nose[3].

1. a quarter of 四分之一
2. in shape 在正常狀態
3. shovel nose
   形狀像鏟子的鼻子
4. trough [trɔːf] (n.) 飼料槽
5. snap [snæp] (v.)
   啪地一聲折斷
6. sink [sɪŋk] (v.) 下沈
7. gaff [gæf] (n.)
   船桅上的斜桁
8. tiller [ˋtɪlə(r)] (n.) 船柄
9. club [klʌb] (n.) 棍；棒
10. as long as 只要

He came like a pig to the trough[4] if a pig had a mouth so wide that you could put your head in it. The old man let him hit the fish and then drove the knife on the oar down into his brain. But the shark jerked backwards as he rolled and the knife blade snapped[5].

The old man did not even watch the big shark sinking[6] slowly in the water.

"I have the gaff[7] now," he said. "But it will do no good. I have the two oars and the tiller[8] and the short club[9]."

Now they have beaten me, he thought.
I am too old to club sharks to death.
But I will try it as long as[10] I have the oars and the short club and the tiller.

It was getting late in the afternoon and he saw
nothing but the sea and the sky.

"You're tired, old man," he said. "You're tired
inside." The sharks did not hit him again until
just before sunset.

He blocked the tiller and reached under the
stern for the club. It was an oar handle[1] from a
broken oar.

The two sharks closed together and as he saw
the one nearest him open his jaws and sink
them into the silver side of the fish,
he raised the club high and brought it down
heavy on the top of the shark's broad[2] head.

He struck[3] the shark once more hard across the point of the nose as he slid down[4] from the fish.

The other shark now came in again with his jaws wide[5]. The old man could see pieces of the meat of the fish spilling[6] white from the corner of his jaws. He swung at him and hit only the head and the shark looked at him and tore[7] the meat loose[8]. The old man swung the club down on him again.

"Come on, *galano*," the old man said. "Come in again."

1. handle [ˋhændl] (n.) 把手
2. broad [brɔːd] (a.) 寬的
3. strike [straɪk] (v.) 攻擊
4. slide down 往下滑
5. with his jaws wide 張大嘴
6. spill [spɪl] (v.) 溢出
7. tear [ter] (v.) 撕裂；扯破 (tear-tore-torn)
8. loose [luːs] (a.) 鬆散的

The shark came in and the old man hit him as he shut[1] his jaws. He hit him solidly[2] and from as high up as he could raise the club. This time he felt the bone[3] at the base[4] of the brain and he hit him again in the same place. The old man watched but neither shark returned.

He did not want to look at the fish. He knew that half of him had been destroyed. The sun had gone down while he had been fighting the sharks.

"It will be dark soon," he said. "Then I should see the glow[5] of Havana. If I am too far to the east I will see the lights of one of the new beaches."

1. shut [ʃʌt] (v.) 閉上；關上
2. solidly [ˋsɑːlɪdli]
   (adv.) 極用力地
3. bone [boʊn] (n.) 骨頭
4. base [beɪs] (n.) 底部；根部
5. glow [gloʊ] (n.) 光輝；發光
6. ruin [ˋruːɪn] (v.) 毀壞
7. something comes into one's head 突然想到某事
8. spear [spɪr] (n.) 魚叉
9. have the luck to . . .
   夠幸運能夠⋯⋯
10. forward [ˋfɔːrwərd]
    (a.) 前面的
11. violate [ˋvaɪəleɪt]
    (v.) 破壞；違反

CHAPTER SIX The Final Battle

He could not talk to the fish anymore because the fish had been ruined[6] too badly. Then something came into his head[7].

"Half-fish," he said. "Fish that you were. I am sorry that I went too far out. I ruined us both. But we have killed many sharks, you and I, and ruined many others. How many did you ever kill, old fish? You do not have that spear[8] on your head for nothing."

I have half of him, he thought. Maybe I'll have the luck to[9] bring the forward[10] half in. I should have some luck. No, he said. You violated[11] your luck when you went too far outside.

"Don't be silly," he said aloud. "You may have much luck yet. I'd like to buy some if there were any place they sell it," he said.

What could I buy it with? he asked himself. Could I buy it with a lost harpoon and a broken knife and two bad hands?

"You might," he said. "You tried to buy it with eighty-four days at sea. They nearly sold it to you too." He saw the reflected[1] glare[2] of the lights of the city at what must have been around ten o'clock at night. He steered[3] inside of the glow and he thought that now, soon, he must hit the edge[4] of the stream[5].

Now it is over, he thought. They will probably hit me again. But what can a man do against them in the dark without a weapon?
I hope I do not have to fight again, he thought.

1. reflected [rɪˋflɛktɪd]
   (a.) 反射的
2. glare [glɛr] (n.) 耀眼的光線
3. steer [stɪr] (v.) 控制航向
4. edge [edʒ] (n.) 邊緣
5. stream [striːm]
   (n.) 潮流；水流
6. useless [ˋjuːsləs]
   (a.) 無作用的
7. in a pack 一群
8. desperately [ˋdɛspərətli]
   (adv.) 絕望地；孤注一擲地
9. seize [siːz] (v.) 攫住；抓住
10. be gone 不見；消失
11. rudder [ˋrʌdə(r)] (n.) 船舵
12. chop [tʃɑːp] (v.) 砍；劈

But by midnight he fought and this time he knew the fight was useless[6]. They came in a pack[7]. He clubbed desperately[8] at what he could only feel and hear and he felt something seize[9] the club and it was gone[10].

He jerked the tiller free from the rudder[11] and beat and chopped[12] with it holding it in both hands and driving it down again and again.

One came, finally, against the head itself and he knew that it was over. He swung the tiller across the shark's head. He swung it once and twice and again. The shark let go[1] and rolled away. That was the last shark of the pack that came. There was nothing more for them to eat.

1. let go 放棄；放手
2. coppery [ˈkɑːpəri] (a.) 銅的
3. be afraid of 恐懼；擔心
4. spit [spɪt] (v.) 吐（唾液等） (spit-spat-spat)
5. remedy [ˈremədi] (n.) 補救
6. notice [ˈnoutɪs] (v.) 注意到
7. along [əˈlɔːŋ] (prep.) 沿著

122

The old man could hardly breathe now and he
felt a strange taste in his mouth. It was coppery[2]
and sweet and he was afraid of[3] it for a moment.
He spat[4] into the ocean and said,
"Eat that, *galanos.*"

He knew he was beaten now finally and
without remedy[5]. He put the sack around his
shoulders and put the skiff on her course.
He had no thoughts nor any feelings of any
kind. He only noticed[6] how lightly and how
well the skiff sailed now that there was no great
weight beside her.

He could feel he was inside the current now and
he could see the lights of the beach along[7] the
shore.

When he sailed into the little harbor the lights of the Terrace were out and he knew everyone was in bed[1]. He pulled the boat up[2] and then he stepped out and tied her to a rock. He took the mast[3] out of its step and furled[4] the sail and tied it. Then he put the mast on his shoulder and started to climb. It was then that he knew the depth of his tiredness[5]. He stopped and looked back and saw the white naked line of the fish's backbone[6] and the dark mass[7] of the head with the bill[8] and all the nakedness[9] in between[10].

He started to climb again and at the top he fell and lay for some time[11] with the mast across his shoulder. He tried to get up. But it was too difficult and he sat there with the mast on his shoulder.

1. be in bed 睡覺
2. pull up 停下
3. mast [mæst] (n.) 船桅
4. furl [fɜːrl] (v.) 捲起；收起
5. tiredness [ˈtaɪərdnəs] (n.) 疲倦
6. backbone [ˈbækboʊn] (n.) 脊骨
7. mass [mæs] (n.) 大塊；大片
8. bill [bɪl] (n.) 喙；鳥嘴
9. nakedness [ˈneɪkɪdnəs] (n.) 赤裸

Finally he put the mast down and stood up.
He picked the mast up and put it on his shoulder
and started up the road. He had to sit down five
times before he reached his shack.

Inside the shack he leaned the mast against the
wall[12]. In the dark he found a water bottle and
took a drink. Then he lay down on the bed.
He pulled the blanket over his body[13] and he
slept face down on the newspapers with his
arms out straight and the palms[14] of his hands
up.

He was asleep when the boy looked in the door
in the morning. The boy saw the old man's
hands and he started to cry. He
went out very quietly to get
some coffee and all the way
down the road he was crying.

10. in between 中間
11. for some time 一小段時間
12. lean A against the wall
    把 A 靠在牆上
13. pull the blanket over one's
    body 拉條毯子蓋在身上
14. palm [pɑːm] (n.) 手心

Many fishermen were around the skiff looking at what was lashed beside it and one was in the water, his trousers rolled up[1], measuring[2] the skeleton[3].

The boy did not go down. He had been there before and one of the fishermen was looking after[4] the skiff for him.

1. roll up 捲起來
2. measure [ˈmeʒə(r)] (v.) 測量
3. skeleton [ˈskelɪtn] (n.) 骸骨
4. look after 看顧
5. disturb [dɪˈstɜːrb] (v.) 打擾

"How is he?" one of the fishermen shouted.
"Sleeping," the boy called. He did not care that
they saw him crying. "Let no one disturb[5] him."
"He was eighteen feet from nose to tail," the
fisherman who was measuring him called.
"I believe it," the boy said.

He went into the Terrace and asked for[6] a can of
coffee.
"Hot and with plenty of milk and sugar in it."
"Anything more?"
"No. Afterwards[7] I will see what he can eat."
"What a fish it was," the proprietor[8] said.
"There has never been such a fish.
Tell him how sorry I am."
"Thanks," the boy said.

6. ask for 要求
7. afterwards ['æftərwərdz]
   (adv.) 之後
8. proprietor [prə`praɪətə(r)]
   (n.) 經營者；所有人

The boy carried the hot can of coffee up to the old man's shack and sat by[1] him until he woke. Finally the old man woke.

"Don't sit up[2]," the boy said. "Drink this."
He poured[3] some of the coffee in a glass.

The old man took it and drank it.
"They beat me, Manolin," he said. "They truly beat me."
"He didn't beat you. Not the fish."
"No. Truly. It was afterwards."
"Pedrico is looking after the skiff and the gear[4]. What do you want done with the head?"
"Let Pedrico chop it up[5] to use in fish traps[6]."
"And the spear[7]?"
"You keep[8] it if you want it."

1. sit by 坐在……旁邊
2. sit up 坐起身子
3. pour [pɔː(r)] (v.) 倒；灌
4. gear [ɡɪr] (n.) 工具
5. chop up 切碎
6. trap [træp] (n.) 陷阱
7. spear [spɪr] (n.) 魚叉
8. keep [kiːp] (v.) 留著
9. search for 搜尋；尋找
10. coast guard 海岸巡邏隊

"I want it," the boy said. "Now we must make
our plans about the other things."
"Did they search for[9] me?"
"Of course. With coast guard[10] and with planes."

"The ocean is very big and a skiff is small and hard to see," the old man said.
He noticed how pleasant it was to have someone to talk to instead of[1] speaking only to himself and to the sea.

"I missed you," he said. "What did you catch?"
"One the first day. One the second and two the third."
"Very good."
"Now we can fish together again."
"No, I am not lucky, I am not lucky anymore."
"The hell[2] with luck," the boy said, "I'll bring the luck with me."
"What will your family say?"

1. instead of 替代地
2. hell [hel] (int.)
   （咒罵語）該死；混蛋
3. have much to learn
   還有很多要學
4. chest [tʃest] (n.) 胸膛
5. lie down 躺下
6. bring [brːŋ] (v.) 帶來
   (bring-brought-brought)

"I do not care. I caught two yesterday. But we will fish together now for I still have much to learn[3]. You get your hands well, old man."

"I know how to care for them. In the night I spat something strange and felt something in my chest[4] was broken."

"Get that well too," the boy said. "Lie down[5], old man. I will bring[6] you your clean shirt. And something to eat."

"Bring any of the papers of the time that I was gone," the old man said.

"You must get well[1] fast for there is much that I can learn and you can teach me everything. How much did you suffer?"

"Plenty," the old man said.

"I'll bring the food and the papers," the boy said. "Rest well, old man. I will bring something from the drugstore[2] for your hands."

As the boy went out the door and down the road he was crying again.

That afternoon there was a party of[3] tourists at the Terrace and looking down in the water among the empty beer cans and dead barracudas[4] a woman saw a great long white spine[5] with a huge tail at the end that lifted and swung with the tide[6].

1. get well 恢復健康
2. drugstore [ˋdrʌgstɔː(r)] (n.) 藥局
3. a party of . . .
   ……的舞會
4. barracuda [ˌbærəˋkuːdə] (n.) 梭魚
5. spine [spaɪn] (n.) 脊椎
6. tide [taɪd] (n.) 潮汐；浪潮
7. garbage [ˋgɑːrbɪdʒ] (n.) 垃圾
8. eshark = a shark
   一隻鯊魚

"What's that?" she asked a waiter and pointed to the long backbone of the great fish that was now just garbage[7] waiting to go out with the tide.

"Tiburon," the waiter said, "Eshark[8]." He wanted to explain what had happened.
"I didn't know sharks had such handsome, beautifully formed[9] tails."
"I didn't either," her male companion[10] said.

Up the road, in his shack, the old man was sleeping again. He was still sleeping on his face[11] and the boy was sitting by him watching him. The old man was dreaming about the lions.

9. form [fɔːrm] (v.)
   構造；成形
10. companion [kəm`paniən]
    (n.) 伙伴；同伴

11. sleep on one's face
    面朝下睡覺

Comprehension Quiz

A True or False.

❶ The old man killed the fish with a harpoon. T F

❷ The big fish was 20 feet long from nose to tail. T F

❸ While the old man was gone, the boy caught four fish. T F

❹ No one searched for the old man while he was gone. T F

❺ The other fishermen felt very sorry for the old man. T F

B Fill in the blanks with the given words.

harbor   violated   pack   jaws   swallowed

❶ The old man _____ his luck by going too far out to sea.

❷ The sharks _____ large parts of the fish with each bite.

❸ The old man tried to get back to the _____ with his fish.

❹ During the night, the sharks attacked in a _____.

❺ The _____ of a shark are terrible.

C Choose the correct answer.

1 What did the boy want to do now that the old man was back?

(a) He wanted to fix dinner for the old man.

(b) He wanted to go fishing with the old man.

(c) He wanted the newspaper to write a story about the old man.

(d) He wanted to go to a baseball game with the old man.

2 What happened to the old man during the last night in the sea?

(a) The old man fell asleep.

(b) The lights of Havana scared the sharks away.

(c) The other fishermen found the old man.

(d) A pack of sharks attacked the old man.

D Match.

1 mako shark • • ⓐ attacked in a pair, bad-smelling, hunters and scavengers

2 galano shark • • ⓑ fast, beautiful except for its long, finger-like teeth

3 shovel-nose shark • • ⓒ like a pig with a mouth wide enough for a person's head

Appendixes

Guide to Listening Comprehension

■ *When listening to the story, use some of the techniques shown below. If you take time to study some phonetic characteristics of English, listening will be easier.*

Get in the flow of English.

English creates a rhythm formed by combinations of strong and weak stress intonations. Each word has its particular stress that combines with other words to form the overall pattern of stress or rhythm in a particular sentence.

When speaking and listening to English, it is essential to get in the flow of the rhythm of English. It takes a lot of practice to get used to such a rhythm. So, you need to start by identifying the stressed syllable in a word.

Listen for the strongly stressed words and phrases.

In English, key words and phrases that are essential to the meaning of a sentence are stressed louder. Therefore, pay attention to the words stressed with a higher pitch. When listening to an English recording for the first time, what matters most is to listen for a general understanding of what you hear. Do not try to hear every single word. Most of the unstressed words are articles or auxiliary verbs, which don't play an important role in the general context. At this level, you can ignore them.

Pay attention to liaisons.

In reading English, words are written with a space between them. There isn't such an obvious guide when it comes to listening to English. In oral English, there are many cases when the sounds of words are linked with adjacent words.

For instance, let's think about the phrase "take off," which can be used in "take off your clothes." "Take off your clothes" doesn't sound like [teɪk ɔːf] with each of the words completely and clearly separated from the others. Instead, it sounds as if almost all the words in context are slurred together, [ˈteɪkɔːf], for a more natural sound.

Shadow the voice of the native speaker.

Finally, you need to mimic the voice of the native speaker. Once you are sure you know how to pronounce all the words in a sentence, try to repeat them like an echo. Listen to the book again, but this time you should try a fun exercise while listening to the English.

This exercise is called "shadowing." The word "shadow" means a dark shade that is formed on a surface. When used as a verb, the word refers to the action of following someone or something like a shadow. In this exercise, pretend you are a parrot and try to shadow the voice of the native speaker.

Try to mimic the reader's voice by speaking at the same speed, with the same strong and weak stresses on words, and pausing or stopping at the same points.

Experts have already proven this technique to be effective. If you practice this shadowing exercise, your English speaking and listening skills will improve by leaps and bounds. While shadowing the native speaker, don't forget to pay attention to the meaning of each phrase and sentence.

Step 1 Listen to what you want to shadow many times. Start out by just trying to shadow a few words or a sentence.

Step 2 Mimic the CD out loud. You can shadow everything the speaker says as if you are singing a round, or you also can speak simultaneously with the recorded voice of the native speaker.

Step 3 As you practice more, try to shadow more. For instance, shadow a whole sentence or paragraph instead of just a few words.

APPENDIX ❷

Listening Guide

CHAPTER ONE : page 10-11

He (❶) ( ) ( ) ( ) who fished alone in a skiff in the Gulf Stream and he had gone (❷) days without catching a fish. During the first forty days (❸) ( ) ( ) the boy's parents had told him that the old man was now ( ) *salao* – the worst form of unlucky. The boy's parents had ordered him to go in another boat which caught three good fish the first week. It made the boy sad to see the old man come back each day with (❹) ( ) empty. He always (❺) ( ) to help him carry the lines, or the gaff and harpoon and the sail patched with flour sacks, so that when it was furled it looked like the flag of permanent defeat.

以下為《老人與海》各章節的前半部。一開始若能聽清楚發音，之後就沒有聽力的負擔。首先，請聽過摘錄的章節，之後再反覆聆聽括弧內單字的發音，並仔細閱讀各種發音的說明。

以下都是以英語的典型發音為基礎，所做的簡易說明，即使這裡未提到的發音，也可以配合CD反覆聆聽，如此一來聽力必能更上層樓。

❶ was an old man: was 的 -s 和其後的 an 連接，聽起來就像是 wasn 的連音；old 和 man 連在一起唸時，old 的 [d] 音會迅速略過，聽起來像是沒有發音。

❷ eighty-four: eighty 的 -t- 因前後皆為有聲母音，因此會發出類似 [d] 的有聲子音，在口語或對話時需特別注意發音；對許多英語學習者而言，eighty 和 eighteen 的發音也常常被搞混，但是可以重音的位置來判斷，eighty 的重音在第一音節，eighteen 的重音在第二音節，且 -teen 發音 [iːn]，可以此分辨兩者。

❸ without a fish: without 的重音在 -out 的部分，因此字首的 wi 發音相當微弱，但是如果要特別強調「沒有」的時候，without a fish 每個音節都要清楚發音。

❹ definitely: definitely 在本句中為強調用語，重音放在第一音節，至於 -t- 與後面的 -ly 連在一起發音時，[t] 音會極不明顯，聽起來像沒有發音。

❺ his skiff: his 和 skiff 相連，兩個 s 只發音一次，當相同的音連在一起，就不會各自單獨發音。

❻ went down: went 的 -t 與 down 連在一起發音時，[t] 會省略不發音，為美語發音的特徵。

The old man was thin and gaunt (①) ( ) ( )
on the back of his neck and deep scars on his hands from
handling lines of heavy fish.

The (②) ( ) ( ) the benign skin cancer that
the tropical sun brings were on his cheeks. His scars were
as old as forgotten memories.

Everything about him was old (③) ( ) ( ).
They were the same color as the sea and were cheerful
and undefeated.

"Santiago," the boy said to him, "(④) ( ) ( )
( ) ( ) again. We've made some money." The old
man had taught the boy to fish and the boy loved him.

"No," the old man said. "You're with a lucky boat.
(⑤) ( )."

"But remember how you went eighty-seven days without
fish and then we caught big ones every day for three
weeks."

"I remember," the old man said. "I know you (⑥)
( ) ( ) me because you doubted."

1 **with deep wrinkles:** 重音放在 deep 這個字，with 的 -th 發 [θ] 音，但在不強調的時候往往不會清楚地發出該音，故聽起來就像 wi 的音，可由前後文判斷正確的單字。

2 **dark spot of:** dark 的 -k 與 spot 連在一起時，[k] 的發音會迅速略過，重音放在 spots 上，而 spots 和 of 連在一起時，of 會變化成 a 的輕音，並與 spot 形成連音。

3 **except his eyes:** except 和 his 連在一起時，his 的 [h] 音消失變成連音，通常以 h 開頭的代名詞（如 he、him、his、her）或助動詞（如 have、had 等），在發弱音時 [h] 因會略過聽不見。

4 **I could go with you:** could 以及發音類似的助動詞 should、would 等，字尾的 [d] 音通常發很輕的音，必須仔細專注才能聽的見。

5 **stay there:** stay 的 -t- 發有聲子音，通常 s 後面若緊接著 [p]、[t]、[k] 等音，就會出現接近沒有氣音的有聲子音。

6 **did not leave:** did 與 not 連在一起發音時，第二個 [d] 音會省略，與 not 一起發連音。

Listening Comprehension

A True or False.

1. _____ T F
2. _____ T F
3. _____ T F
4. _____ T F
5. _____ T F
6. _____ T F

B Listen to the CD and choose the correct answer.

1. _____?

   (a) How to catch a big fish.

   (b) How an old man overcame an unlucky streak.

   (c) How an old man proves that he can still catch fish.

2. _____?

   (a) He won a very long arm-wrestling match.

   (b) He was a great baseball player.

   (c) He always caught the biggest fish.

C Listen to the CD and fill in the blanks.

1 It made the boy sad to see the old man come back each day with his _____ _____.

2 There was no cast net, but they went _____ _____ _____ every day.

3 He was _____ _____ and it was no effort for him.

4 He is a great fish but I must _____ him that he is _____ _____ for me.

5 If you do not sleep you might become _____ in the head.

6 The old man felt _____ _____ _____ and he could not see well.

D Listen to the CD and write down the sentences. Rearrange the sentences in chronological order.

1 _____

2 _____

3 _____

4 _____

5 _____

_____ ⇨ _____ ⇨ _____ ⇨ _____ ⇨ _____

中　譯

p. 8 老人

　　我一生以捕魚為業，我現在年紀很大了，但是身體依然硬朗，意志也很堅決。我非常精通捕魚，這也代表我有很豐富的捕魚知識，但是最近我已經好幾個星期沒有魚獲了，我知道我很快就會再捕到魚，所以我每天乘船出海垂釣。

男孩

　　我住在哈瓦那，離其他漁民居住的海灘很近。我很小的時候就學會捕魚，老人教會我捕魚的一切知識。他是個很棒的人，但我父母卻認為他是個不祥之人。我相信他有一天終會再捕到大魚。

p. 10-11
[第1章] 極度的厄運

　　在墨西哥灣流中，他是一名駕著小船獨自捕魚的老人。他已經連續八十四毫無漁獲了。在第四十天的時候，小男孩的父母告訴他，老人現在無疑就是「salao」，意思是運氣背到極點。男孩的父母要他跟著另一艘船出海，那艘船出海第一週就捕到三條上等的大魚。看著老人每天駕著空蕩蕩的小艇回航，男孩很難過，他總是會過去幫忙老人扛起魚線、魚鉤、魚叉等魚具，以及滿是麵粉袋補丁的

146

船帆，當這片帆布收捲起來時，看起來就像是一面象徵著注定要失敗的旗幟。

老人的身形清癯瘦削，頸部後方有一道道深烙的皺紋，雙手也因捕到大魚時拉扯魚線，留下了一條條深深的疤痕。他的臉頰上布滿深色斑點，那是熱帶地區的炙熱陽光造成的良性皮膚腫瘤。他雙手上的舊疤當時是怎麼留下來的，已不復記憶。

他身上的一切都是蒼老的，除了那一雙眼睛。他的雙眼湛藍如海，神采奕奕，一副不屈不撓的樣子。

`p. 12-13` 「桑堤亞戈，」 男孩對老人說：「我可以再跟你一起出海，以前我們也一起賺了些錢的。」

過去他教導男孩捕魚，小男孩非常敬愛他。

「不，」老人說，「你跟了一艘幸運的漁船，繼續待在那兒吧。」

「但是你還記得嗎？那時候你連續八十七天都沒捕到魚，接下來的三個星期，我們每天都捕到了大魚。」

「我記得。」老人說，「我知道你不是不信任我的技術而離開的。」

「是爸爸叫我去的，我只是個小孩，我得聽他的。」

「我明白。」老人說。

「他的信心不夠。」

「沒錯，但是我們有，不是嗎？」

「是的。我可以先請你去露臺酒館喝杯啤酒，然後再把這些工具搬回家嗎？」

「好啊。」老人說，「漁夫之間的小酌。」

p. 14-15 他們坐在酒館裡，許多漁夫取笑老人，但老人並不以為意。年紀大一點的漁夫看著老人，心裡為他感到難過，但是都沒有把這種情緒表現出來。那一天大豐收的漁夫們都已經把魚切好，準備搬上放滿冰塊的卡車，運回哈瓦那市場去。至於那些捕到鯊魚的漁夫，則把鯊魚運到海灣另一邊的鯊魚工廠去。當風自東方吹來，也從鯊魚工廠帶來一陣魚腥味。

「桑堤亞戈。」男孩喊道。

「嗯？」老人回答，他心中浮現多年前的回憶。

「我能不能去幫你準備些明天要用來當餌的沙丁魚？」

「不行，你去打棒球吧！我還有力氣划船，羅傑利會幫我撒網。」

「我想要幫你做，就算我不能和你一起捕魚，也希望能幫點忙。」

「你已經請我喝啤酒了啊！」老人說道：「你現在是個大人了！」

「我第一次和你一起上船的時候幾歲？」

「五歲，我太早把一隻魚拖上船，差點害你丟了小命，船也幾乎給毀了，你還記得嗎？」

p. 16-17 「我還記得那條魚的尾巴甩個不停，還有那陣拍打的聲音。」

「你真的記得嗎？」

「我記得我們一起捕魚的每一件事。」

老人看著他，眼神充滿驕傲與慈祥，「如果你是我的孩子，我會帶你一起出海，」他說，「但是你是你父母的孩子，而且你現在跟的船正在走運。」

「那我能幫你準備些沙丁魚嗎？我還知道哪裡能找到四種魚餌。」

「我今天還有剩下一些。」

「我去幫你準備四個新鮮的魚餌。」

「一個就夠了。」老人說道，他一直都深具希望與信心的。

「兩個。」男孩說。

「那就兩個吧。」老人同意了，「你不是偷來的吧？」

「我是可以偷，」男孩說，「不過這些是我買的。」

「謝謝，」老人說，「由這股潮流來看，明天應該會是豐收的一天。」他的想法太單純，壓根沒想過自己何時應該學會謙遜。不過他深知，即使擁有驕傲自信也沒什麼損失。

「你明天要去哪裡？」男孩問。

「很遠的地方，我想要在日出前就出海。」

p. 18-19 「你現在還有力氣捕很大的魚嗎？」

「我想可以，我懂得很多技巧。」

「我們把這些工具拿回家吧。」男孩說，「我可以去拿漁網捕些沙丁魚。」

他們拾起船上的用具，老人把船杆扛在肩上，男孩拿起裝著各種捕魚工具的木箱。

他們一起走到老人的小屋，穿過敞開的大門，小屋是用大王椰子樹最堅硬的枝幹建造的。

小屋裡有一張床、一張桌子，一張椅子，在滿是灰塵的地板上，有個角落用來燒炭煮東西。在棕褐色的牆上，掛著一幅彩色的耶穌聖像以及一幅聖母圖，兩樣都是老人妻子的遺物。過去牆上本來還掛著他妻子的照片，但後來老人把它拿了下來，因為那張照片總讓他備感孤寂，現在那張照片收在角落的架子裡，擺在他洗乾淨的襯衫底下。

p. 20-21 「你要吃什麼？」男孩問。

「一鍋黃米飯配魚吃，你要不要也來一點？」

「不用了，我等一下要回家吃飯，要

我幫你生個火嗎？」

「沒關係，我等一下自己弄就好。」

「我可以拿漁網嗎？」

「當然。」

但是男孩知道老人家裡根本就沒有漁網，他還記得漁網是什麼時候被賣掉的，他們每天就這麼假裝演戲，當然也沒有那一鍋黃米飯和魚，男孩心知肚明。

「85是個幸運數字。」老人說，「要是我捕到一條超過千磅重的大魚回來，你應該會很高興吧？」

「我去拿網捕些沙丁魚，你要坐在門口曬曬太陽嗎？」

「好啊，我有昨天的報紙，我要來看看棒球的消息。」

男孩不知道他是不是真有昨天的報紙，不過老人真的從床鋪底下拿出來了。

「培利戈在酒館拿給我的。」老人解釋道。

「我捕到沙丁魚就回來，我會把你的那一分和我的一起擺在冰上，明天早上我們可以一起用，等我回來你也可以跟我說些棒球的消息。記得要保暖啊，老先生，現在已經是九月分了呢。」男孩說。

「是上等魚貨出現的月份，」老人說，「而在五月，誰都有能耐當漁夫。」

「我要去捕沙丁魚了。」男孩說。

p. 22-23 男孩回來的時候，老人已經在椅子上睡著，太陽也已經下山了，男孩從床上拿下破舊的軍毯，鋪在椅背上，讓它覆蓋著老人形狀奇特但有力的肩膀上。老人襯衫上的補丁太多，看起來就像一張帆，他的臉十分蒼老，閉起眼睛時似乎毫無血色，兩條腿打著赤腳。

男孩沒有吵醒老人，等他再回來，老人依然沈睡。

「醒醒啊，老先生。」男孩說。

老人張開眼睛，他神情恍惚

一會兒才清醒過來。他笑著問道：「你捕到些什麼？」

「晚餐，」男孩說，「我們來吃晚餐吧。」

「我不怎麼餓。」

「來吃一些吧，你不能光捕魚不吃飯。」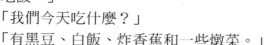

「我們今天吃什麼？」

「有黑豆、白飯、炸香蕉和一些燉菜。」

p. 24-25 這些食物是男孩從露臺酒館的鍋裡拿的。

「你真是好心，」老人說，「我們來吃吧！」

「我就是要叫你來吃飯的，」男孩輕聲說道，「我想等你要吃的時候再把蓋子打開。」

「我要吃了，」老人說，「只是我得先洗個手。」

「他要去哪兒洗啊？」男孩想。村裡供應的水位在兩條街外，我應該幫他提些水過來，還有香皂、毛巾。我怎麼會這麼粗心呢？我還得幫他準備一件襯衫和夾克在冬天禦寒，再準備一些鞋子和一條毯子。

「你的燉菜味道好極了！」老人說。

「跟我說說棒球的消息。」男孩問他。

「就像我之前說的，美國大聯盟最值得一瞧的就是洋基隊。」

「他們今天輸了！」男孩對他說。

「那沒什麼大不了的，偉大的狄馬喬又重振雄風了。」

「他們隊裡還有其他人。」

「是沒錯，但是有他在可就不一樣了。」老人說，「你還記得他以前去過露臺酒館嗎？我本來想邀他去釣魚，不過不好意思開口，後來我叫你去幫我問，你也害羞不敢問。我想帶偉大的狄馬喬去釣魚，聽說他父親也是漁夫，說不定也和我們一樣窮，能夠了解我們的狀況。

我曾經跟過一艘大船上，航行到非洲，傍晚時還在海邊看到了獅子。」

「我知道，你跟我說過。」

p. 26-27 「我們是在討論非洲還是棒球？」

「棒球，跟我說說麥葛洛的事。」男孩說。

「過去那段日子他有時候會出現在露臺酒館，不過他要是一喝太多，行為和言語就會失態。」

「那麼說真的，誰是最棒的經紀人，是魯基還是龔薩雷茲？」

「我覺得他們旗鼓相當。」

「至於最棒的漁夫，就是你。」

「不是，我知道有人比我更好。」

「你怎麼能這麼說？」男孩說道，「其他漁夫可能不錯，或許有一些真的很棒，但你就這麼一個！」

「謝謝你，逗我開心。希望我釣到的魚不要太大，免得證明我們錯了。」

「你的力氣要是還像你說的那樣大，那再大的魚也不怕。」

「我可能已經不再那麼有力氣了，」老人說，「但我懂得很多捕魚的技巧，我還有堅定的決心。」

p. 28-29 「你該上床睡覺了，這樣明天早上才會有精神。」

「晚安！我明天早上會叫你起床。」

「你就是我的鬧鐘。」男孩說。

「我的鬧鐘就是我的年紀，」老人說，「為什麼老人家總是一大早就醒？難道是為了醒著活久一點？」

「我不知道，」男孩說，「我只知道年輕人可以睡得很晚很熟。晚安囉，老先生！」

他們吃飯的時候桌上並沒有燈，老人把他的一條褲子捲起來，把報紙塞在裡面當枕頭，接著他將整個身體蜷縮在毯子下，身體底下的是鋪在彈簧床上的舊報紙。

海明威及《老人與海》

在海明威寫《老人與海》時，他自己也已經邁入老年。他的前一本書並非佳作，但是《老人與海》一推出卻空前成功。海明威使用簡潔精鍊的語言來描寫一位老人的堅定，再次緊緊抓住全世界讀者的心。有些人認爲海明威其實是在描寫他自己，想要再一嚐成功作家的滋味。

很多人認爲老人一角取材自葛瑞格‧富安帝斯，一名爲海明威工作的古巴人。在海明威居住於古巴期間，富安帝斯是他所擁有的漁船「Pilar號」的船長。

不過，富安帝斯曾對記者提出不同的說法，某天他與海明威乘坐在Pilar號時，他們看見一位老漁夫，老漁夫坐在一艘小船上，船緣掛著一條大魚，海明威對富安帝斯說他想要寫關於這個漁夫的故事。

這個故事可能是海明威結合自己與朋友的故事，再加上他所見的人物而創作的。這也可能是本故事能感動那麼多讀者的原因，因爲老人的角色正好反應了那些努力不懈、決心要再獲得成功的人。

[第2章] 深入遠洋

老人在睡夢中見到了兒時的非洲與長長的金色海灘，那時他每晚獨自住在岸邊，在夢裡，他聽見海潮聲，也見到隨著海浪而來的當地船隻。睡夢中，他嗅到了清晨微風帶來的非洲氣息。

他已不再夢見暴風雨，不再夢見女人，不再夢見什麼了不起的大事，也不再夢到大魚、打鬥、和人比力氣這些事，甚至不再夢見亡妻。如今他只夢見那個有獅子的海灘，獅子們就像小貓一樣在泥濘中玩耍。他愛這群獅子就如同愛小男孩一般，但是他從未夢見過男孩。

現在他醒過來，看著月光下敞開的大門，他把捲起的褲子攤平後穿上，動身去把小男孩叫醒，男孩家的門沒有鎖，老人打開門靜靜走了進去，他輕輕抓著男孩的腳，直到男孩醒過來，轉身看著他。老人點點頭，男孩抓起掛在床邊椅子上長褲，坐在床上穿起來。

`p. 34-35` 老人走出門口，男孩在後面跟著他，他還是很想睡，老人搭著他的肩膀說道：「我很抱歉。」

「有什麼好抱歉的。」男孩說：「這本來就是男人的工作。」

他們走向老人的小屋，在昏暗的天色下，一路上盡是光著腳的男人，扛著自己船上的桅杆。

他們到了老人的小屋後，男孩從籃子裡拿出成捲的繩索、魚叉和魚鉤，老人則把船桅和捲起的船帆扛在肩上。

「你要喝點咖啡嗎？」男孩問。

「我們先把工具放到船上，再去喝點咖啡。」

他們來到一個清晨供應漁民餐點的地方，喝了些加了濃縮牛奶的咖啡。

「你睡得好嗎，老先生？」男孩問。男孩雖然還是有點想睡，但是他現在已經完全清醒。

`p. 36-37` 「非常好，瑪諾里，」老人說，「我今天很有信心。」

「我也是，」男孩說，「現在我來分配沙丁魚，給你些新鮮的魚餌。

我馬上就回來，」男孩說，「再喝杯咖啡，這裡可以賒帳。」

　　老人慢慢喝著咖啡，這將是他今天一整天唯一的食物，他知道應該把它喝完。長久以來他不熱衷飲食，也從不帶著午餐出海，他在小船邊放了一瓶水，那就是他一整天唯一需要的食物。

　　這時男孩帶著沙丁魚和兩個魚餌回來，他們踏上小船，腳下踩的是帶著石粒的細沙。他們解開纜繩，把小船划向海中。

　　「祝你好運，老先生。」

　　「也祝你好運！」老人回道。

　　他把船槳用繩索固定在船橡的槳座上，身子往前傾，開始離開岸邊，往更陰暗的海面划去。除了老人以外，還有其他船隻前進大海，雖然老人看不到他們，但還是可以聽到船槳碰到水面往前推進的聲音。

p. 38-39 老人知道這次他將航向遙遠的外海，土地的氣息他已然拋到腦後，只管划向清晨嶄新的海洋香氣。

　　他身處一片黑暗之中，但他可以感覺到白晝即將來臨。划著船的同時，他聽到飛魚躍出水面的聲音。他很喜歡飛魚，牠們是他在大海中最忠實的朋友，但他也很同情飛鳥，特別是那些黑色的小巧燕鷗，牠們不斷飛行尋找著食物，卻常常一無所獲。老人心想：「鳥兒過著比人類更加辛苦的生活，除了那些搶奪食物和長得又大又壯的飛鳥。為什麼創造出像海鷗那麼細緻美麗的鳥，卻又讓牠們生活在大海這個嚴苛的環境裡？大海雖然寬廣美麗，但也是非常無情的。」

　　他總是把大海想成他的「la mar」，在西班牙文中，這是對愛人的稱呼。那些熱愛大海的人也有時不免數落大海，而且在口氣上都把大海當成女人來看待。一些開著汽艇的年輕漁夫會將大海視為男性，提到大海的時候，就把它想成競爭對手甚至是對立的敵人。但是老人總把大海想成女性，她有時會略施恩惠，有時卻又不假辭色，要是她做了什麼瘋狂或邪惡的事，完全是因為她無法克制自己。他認為月亮的變化盈缺影響著她，一如影響著婦女一樣。

p. 40-41 他平穩地往前划，沒花什麼力氣。

「今天我要划到鰹魚和鮪魚群聚集處，說不定會有大魚隨著魚群出現。」

在天還未大亮之前，他隨著水流，將四個餌分別放在四個不同的深度，魚鉤上的每個一部分都會讓大魚感覺鮮甜可口。

他把男孩給他的兩條新鮮小鮪魚纏在最深的兩條魚線上，另外兩條魚線上則分別勾著大條的藍色參魚和黃色雄鮭。每一條魚線都和筆一樣粗，纏繞在一條棍子上，只要有魚拉到或是碰到魚餌，棍子就會往下沈。

老人緩緩划著小船，讓魚線保持垂直，並維持在適當的高度。薄薄的陽光從海面升起，讓老人能夠看見其他船隻在水中以低速朝岸邊前進。他低下頭看著水面，看著筆直落在水中的魚線，他能讓魚線垂直的程度更勝其他漁夫。

「我讓魚線維持精確的垂直度，」他想，「因為只有我完全不能靠運氣捕到魚。」但誰說得準呢？說不定今天正是我的幸運日，畢竟每天都是個嶄新的開始，運氣佳固然不錯，不過還是把一切做到最好、最準確，那麼當運氣來敲門時，你就已經做好準備了。

就在這時，他看見一隻軍艦鳥伸展著長長的翅膀在前方的空中盤旋，急速往海面俯衝，接著繼續在空中盤旋。

p. 42 「牠捕到獵物了，」老人大聲地對自己說道，「牠不光是旁觀而已。」

「是海豚，」老人大聲說，「是隻大海豚。」

老人看著軍艦鳥的同時，一條小鮪魚浮出海面，轉了一圈又回到水中，接下來一隻接著一隻的鮪魚在魚餌後方高高跳起，過了一段時間，放在小船尾端的魚線在他腳下被緊緊拉動了。

老人趕緊放下槳，並感覺到小鮪魚拉扯魚線的重量，當他將魚線往船上拉的時候，還能看見水中青綠色的魚背，老人出於仁慈敲了敲牠的頭，接著便把小鮪魚放回船下的魚群裡。

p. 44-45 「青花魚類，」老人高聲說著，「很棒的魚餌。」

他不記得自己從何時開始有了這種自言自語的習慣，可能是從小男孩不和他一起出海之後，不過他自己也不記得了。

此刻天氣變得炎熱，老人可以感覺到陽光就這麼照在他的頸背上。他划著船，感覺到汗珠就從他的背上滴落。這時他看到其中一條綠色的線劇烈地擺動。

「太好了！」他說，「太好了！」他收回船槳，伸手握住魚線，用右手拇指與食指精確地控制魚線。

魚線再次晃動，這回並不是猛力的拉扯，老人完全知道這代表什麼：水深六百呎處一條槍魚正吃著魚鉤上的沙丁魚。

太棒了！這肯定是條大魚，他心想著。吃吧，魚兒，快吃吧！這時他先察覺到一陣細微的動作，接著是更用力的拉扯，想必是因為沙丁魚的頭鉤在魚鉤上，很難把它從鉤子上扯下來，接著魚線便毫無動靜了。

p. 46-47 「來吧！」老人大聲說道，「聞聞看，味道不錯吧？快吃吧，等一下還有鮪魚！別客氣，魚兒們，吃吧！」接著他感覺到一股沉甸甸而不可思議的重量，那是魚的重量。他先鬆手讓魚線不斷地下沈再下沈，現在，他已做好準備，手中有三綑240呎長的魚線預備著，和沈入海中的魚線一樣長。

「再多吃一點，」他說，「好好地吃啊！」

他想，就吃到魚鉤刺穿你的心臟，奪走性命吧，那時你就會很快浮出水面，讓他可以用魚叉一叉而入。你準備好了嗎？這餐吃夠了嗎？

「就是現在！」他大喊一聲，兩手用力收線，拉回了約一碼長的魚線，接著再繼續不斷地拉，使盡手臂與全身的力量地拉著魚線。

但什麼事也沒發生！大魚只管緩緩游著，老人絲毫無法拉動牠。小船繼續慢慢朝西北方駛去，魚群平順地游開，步調緩慢地在平靜的海水裡悠游。

「真希望小男孩有和我一起出海。」老人大聲地說，「現在我竟然被魚拖著跑，我要把我會的都教給他，只要他想，我就把魚線交給他。感謝上帝，牠只是游到其他地方，不是沈到海底。」

四小時後，大魚繼續游向外海，拖著小艇，老人則緊緊握著纏繞背後的漁線不放。

p. 50-51

[第3章] 搏鬥的開始

老人回頭看，發現陸地已遙不可見。但這不礙事，他想。我可以尋哈瓦那的燈火回到陸地上。大魚可能日落前浮上水面，也可能晚上才浮出來。我沒有抽筋，力氣也還很大，被魚鉤勾住嘴的是牠，不是我，不過，能這麼拉扯魚線的魚可不簡單，真希望能親眼看看在我面前的是什麼魚。

大魚一直沒有改變游向，太陽下山後，天氣轉冷，老人把蓋在裝魚餌桶子上的麻袋披在脖子上，覆蓋至背部。魚線繞在他的肩膀上，他小心翼翼把麻袋披在魚線下方。

　　我對牠無計可施，牠也拿我無可奈何，他想。有這麼一回，他站起身在船邊小便，一邊看著天上的星星確認前進的方向。現在星辰移動的速度更慢了，哈瓦那的燈火不是很明顯，他曉得海流應該是帶著他們航向東方。

p. 52-53 不知道今天大聯盟棒球比賽的結果如何，他想，要是能邊捕魚邊聽收音機，不知道有多好。但想想你正在做的工作吧，沒能閒混的！

　　接著他又大聲說：「我真希望小男孩跟著我，幫忙我，看著這條魚。」

　　他想，人老了是不應該孤伶伶的，但這卻是無法避免的。我得記得在鮪魚發臭之前吃了它，保持一點力氣，千萬要記得，在天亮前把鮪魚吃掉，他對自己說。

　　到了晚上，兩隻海豚游到小船邊，老人可以聽見牠們在附近旋轉鳴叫。

　　「牠們挺可愛的，」他說，「牠們嬉戲玩樂，彼此相親相愛，就像飛魚一樣是我們漁夫的好朋友。」

p. 54-55 接著他開始為自己鉤住的大魚感到難過。牠很了不奇，很不可思議，不知道牠年紀多大了，老人不禁想著。我以前沒捕過這麼有力氣的魚，也沒捕過一隻反應這麼特別的魚，說不定牠太聰明了，所以沒有跳。牠只要用力一跳，就能要了我的命。不過這真是一條上等的大魚，要是肉質鮮美的話，在市場不知道能賣多好的價錢啊。牠像男子漢一樣咬下魚餌，扯著魚線，在搏鬥時毫不驚慌，不曉得牠是早有計畫，還是牠根本就是和我一樣都豁出去了。

　　「真希望小男孩也在這兒。」他大聲地說。他身體靠著船頭，從繞著肩膀的魚線感覺到大魚扯著線的力量。我要到無人的地方，把牠揪出來。現在我們同在一條船上，無法得到任何幫助。

　　這時大魚突然掀起一陣大浪，老人被拉跌倒，眼睛下方撞出了一個傷口，少量鮮血從他臉頰滑下，但還沒流到下巴就已經凝結乾涸，接著他又靠在船頭，抵著木造的船身休息。

p. 56-57 不知道牠為什麼突然掀起大浪，他想，應該是魚線滑過牠的背脊，當然牠的背一定不會比我的背更難受，不過就算牠再厲害，也不可能這麼一直拖著小船。

　　「魚啊！」他輕柔地喊著，接著又大聲說：「我會就這麼跟著你，直到我斷氣為止。」

　　當太陽從遠處升起，老人明白大魚還沒疲倦，只有一個跡象對老人有利，那就是魚線傾斜的程度顯示大魚游在海中的深度變淺了，那就代表牠應該不會跳躍，雖然也不無可能。

　　「上帝啊，請讓牠跳吧，」老人說，「我有足夠的魚線應付牠。」

　　「大魚啊，」他接著說，「我非常敬佩你、欣賞你，但是今天結束之前，我一定要把你解決。」

　　一隻小鳥從北方向小船飛過來，那是鳴禽類的鳥，老人看得出牠非常疲累。牠飛到老人頭頂上打轉，接著便停在魚線上休息。

　　「你年紀多大啦？」老人問小鳥，「這是你的第一次遠行嗎？」小鳥兒實在太累了，細緻的爪子緊勾住魚線，在魚線上搖搖晃晃。

　　「好好休息一下吧，小鳥。」他說，「休息完就啟程，好好抓住你的機會，就像其他人、其他鳥兒或是魚一樣。」

p. 58-59 就在這時，小船被大魚拖得突然傾斜，老人跌坐在船上，要不是放開一點魚線，支撐住自己的身體，他早已經被拖下船了。小鳥嚇得飛走了，他仔細摸索右手握著的魚線，發現手正在流血。他把線的重量改放在左肩上，小心翼翼地彎下腰，用海水清洗右手，傷口的位置正好在他工作需要用到的範圍，他明白在這場戰役結束前必須用到雙手，在一切沒結束前他可不願意再弄傷手。

「現在，」他說，「我得把鮪魚給吃了。」

他跪下拿出放在船尾的鮪魚，用膝部壓著魚，從鮪魚的身體至尾端之間切下幾片深紅色的魚肉。

「我想我應該吃不完整條魚。」他說，感覺到魚線被規律地拉扯著，他的左手抽筋了。

「這算是什麼手？」他說，「要抽筋就抽個夠吧！變成爪子也行，只是那一點好處也沒有。」

他拿起一塊鮪魚放進嘴裡，慢慢地咀嚼著，味道不怎麼好。

「你感覺怎麼樣啊，我的手？」他問著抽筋的左手，左手現在簡直僵硬得像屍體一樣，「我會為了你多吃一點。」

真希望我也能餵餵那條魚，他想，牠就像是我的兄弟一樣，不過我還是得殺了牠，為了達到目的，我必須保持體力。老人慢慢地把鮪魚片全都吃下肚。

「上帝，讓我不要再抽筋了吧。」他說，「不知道這條魚接下來會出什麼招啊。」

牠的計畫到底是什麼？而我又有什麼計畫呢？

p. 60-61 他的左手還是在抽筋，但是已經漸漸好轉。

我痛恨抽筋，他想，那是一種背叛自己身體的舉動。接著，他的右手感受到魚線拉扯的方式不一樣了。

「牠要浮上來了」，他說道，「加油啊，左手，加油！」

161

魚線緩慢而穩定地往上升，接著小船前方的海面突然升起，大魚浮出水面了。牠不斷地出現在海面上，兩側的海水在牠身邊翻滾著。陽光下，牠閃閃發光，牠的頭和身體兩側都很寬闊，是閃閃發亮的淡紫色。魚嘴就和棒球棒一樣長，越往前端越尖銳，牠的身體整個冒出水面，接著又跳入水中，動作順暢地猶如潛水夫。老人看著牠鐮刀形狀的魚尾落入海裡，劃出一道疾速前行的水痕。

　　「牠的身體比小船還長上兩呎。」老人說，他雙手控制著魚線，避免因用力過猛導致魚線斷裂。他心裡明白，要是不能穩定地施加壓力讓這條大魚放慢速度，他就可能用盡並扯斷魚線。

`p. 62-63` 這真是條大魚，不過我得讓牠以為自己沒辦法和我對抗，我決不能讓牠發現自己的力量有多大，更不能讓牠知道要是牠快速往前游會有什麼結果。

　　老人曾經見過許多大魚，也見過不少超過千磅的大魚，甚至曾經捕到過兩條，但都不是在獨自出海的時候。如今他獨自一人在海上，在看不見陸地的遠洋，他被一條從未見過甚至從未聽聞過的大魚急速拖行著，而他的左手還在抽筋呢。

　　不知道牠為什麼要躍出水面？老人納悶，感覺起來，牠跳出來就是要讓我知道牠到底有多大，真希望我能讓牠看看我是個什麼樣的人，不過這樣牠也會看到我的手在抽筋。

　　到了中午，老人的手總算恢復正常，感覺舒服了一點，不過身體依然承受著不小的痛苦，雖然他並不承認自己會痛。

　　「我沒有信教，」他說，「但是我要說十次慈祥的天父，十次萬福瑪麗亞，請保佑我捕到這隻魚，要是讓我抓到牠，我保證一定到聖母面前祭拜。上帝啊！我真不知道牠會有這麼大。」

162

p. 64-65 「不過我會解決牠，」他說，「雖然牠體型巨大。」

或許這是不義的，他想，不過我會讓牠瞧瞧，一個男人能成就什麼事、能有多大的耐力。

「我告訴過小男孩，我是個強壯的老人。」他說，「現在該是證明的時候了。」

無論他過去曾經證明過多少次都不重要，現在他要再次證明自己的能力。

「大魚啊，要是你還不累，」他大聲說著，「你一定是隻奇特的魚。」

老人現在疲累不堪，他努力想些其他的事。他想到了大聯盟，他知道紐約洋基隊正在和底特律老虎隊對打。

今天是比賽的第二天，不知道比賽結果如何了，他想，不過我得有信心，我和偉大的狄馬喬一樣，能完美地達成任何目標。

他想，你相信偉大的狄馬喬會像我一樣，和一條魚耗那麼長的時間嗎？我相信他一定會，甚至可以耗更久，因為他年輕又身強力壯，而且他父親也是一位漁夫呢。

p. 66-67
人類與大自然

從人類在洞穴做壁畫的遠古時期開始，藝術作品便一直深受大自然的影響。自人類開始熟悉大自然之後，便變將其視為競爭對手，或生活所需的供應者。從人類的歷史來看，自然的力量曾經造成極大的災難，奪走不少人命，不論是在陸地或海上，人類都必須不斷奮鬥求生存，而這些奮鬥的過程在不同時代便表現在不同的藝術作品中。

例如貝多芬在第六號交響曲裡表現出雷雨的狂暴劇烈，梅爾維爾的經典文學作品《白鯨記》，細膩地描繪出

人與自然間的對抗，至於海明威的
《老人與海》一書中，也傳達同樣的
主題。

　　不過從另一個角度來看，海明威書中的老人並不是不
斷與自然對抗，自然提供老人生活所需的糧食，即使是一
隻迷途的飛鳥，也在老人孤獨的戰役中提供一點陪伴的溫
暖。老人並沒有將自然視為敵人，反而把大海看作頻頻改
變心情狀態的女性，有時她溫和而慈愛，有時卻是殘忍又
嚴酷。

p. 68-69

[第4章] 公平的戰鬥

　　太陽下山後，老人為了讓自己恢復一點信心，他回憶
起自己曾經在卡薩布蘭加的一間酒館裡，與一名來自古巴
西恩富戈斯、人高馬大的黑人比腕力，那可是整個碼頭上
最強壯的人。

　　他們的手肘從早到晚都沒離開過桌上那條粉筆畫的
線，兩人都極力想把對方的手扳倒，每隔四小時他們就換
裁判，讓別的裁判有時間休息睡覺。

　　　　一整晚比賽雙方僵持不下，黑
人一度只差三吋就能扳倒老人，那
時候的老人可不老，而是冠軍桑堤亞
戈。但老人再次奮力舉起手臂，他相信自己絕對可以打敗
黑人，雖然黑人是個好人，又是個很棒的運動員。到了日
出時，黑人的手一次又一次被他壓倒在桌上，直到那隻手
無力地垂放在桌上。這場比賽從週日上午開始，一直到週
一清晨才告結束。

p. 70-71　很長一段時間每個人都把他稱作「冠軍」，在這場
比賽過後，他又與人比了幾場，接著便沒再比過腕力了。
他知道自己如果下定決心，誰他都能夠打敗，不過為了捕

魚的工作，他也決定不再與人比腕力。

　　接近天黑時，小船駛過一片如小島般的馬尾藻，這時一隻海豚咬住他的一小段魚線，當海豚躍出水面，在海上恣意彎曲擺動著身體，移動至船尾處，老人連忙靠過去，從船尾奮力拉起閃著紫色光芒的金銅色大魚。大魚突然張大嘴咬向魚鉤，用長而光滑的身軀、尾端以及頭部去撞小船底部，一直到老人用船槳敲了牠一下，牠抖了抖身軀，接著便一動也不動。

　　老人看著夕陽落到海平面下，再看看依然斜在前方的粗魚線。

　　「牠完全沒停下來的跡象。」他說，看著自己的手在水中滑行，他發現大魚的速度稍微慢了下來。

 **p. 72-73**　「我要把兩支船槳交叉綁在船尾，這在夜裡可以減慢牠的速度，」他說，「到了晚上牠會變得更能抵抗，不過我也不弱。」

　　我正在學習如何征服大魚，他想，至少學到了一部分，接著他想到，大魚自從上鉤後就沒再吃過東西了，這麼大的一條魚，需要更多的食物。而我呢，已經吃了一整條的鰹魚，明天我要吃那條海豚。

　　「現在覺得如何啊，大魚？」他大聲地問，「我覺得挺不錯的，左手也舒服多了，食物還能撐個一天一夜，繼續拖著船走吧，魚兒。」

　　其實老人並不覺得舒服，交纏在他背後的魚線讓他痛苦不堪，甚至有些麻木，這讓他很擔心。

　　不過更糟的我都經歷過了，他想，現在我的手不過被割傷，另一隻手也不抽筋了，我的雙腿則好的不得了。

　　現在天色已完全暗了下來，時值九月，日落後天黑得特別快，星星已經冒了出來，他看到獵戶座那顆名叫參宿七的星星，雖然不知道它正確的名稱，不過他心裡明白，再過不久其他星星便會冒出頭來，這些遙遠的朋友會陪在他身邊作伴。

p. 74-75 「這條大魚也是我的朋友，」他聲音宏亮地說道，「我從沒見過甚至聽過有這麼大的魚，不過我卻得殺了牠，眞高興我們不必消滅那些星星朋友。」

接著他爲大魚無法進食而感到難過，而即將殺了牠的決心，並沒有減緩他爲大魚感受到的難過。他想，牠能餵飽多少人啊！但是那些人夠資格享用牠嗎？不，當然不夠資格，沒有人夠資格吃一條如此自負的魚。

老人休息了一段時間，大約是兩個小時吧，月亮遲至現在才升起，因此他無從判斷時間。現在他的背依然忍受著大魚拉扯前進的魚線。

「但是你到現在都還沒睡過覺呢，老頭子！都已經過了半天又一夜，馬上又將是新的一天，而你完全沒閤過眼。」他大聲說著，「如果牠一直這麼穩定地前進，我得想個辦法睡一下，要是再不睡一會兒，腦子會變得不清楚的。」

我是可以這麼一直保持清醒，他對自己說，不過這太危險了。

他又回到船的尾端，現在的星星閃爍晶亮，他能清楚地看見那條海豚，他用刀刺向海豚頭部，施力將牠從船尾拉上來。牠的身體已經冰冷，而在星辰的照耀下，顯現銀白色的光芒。老人右腳踏在海豚的頭上，開始剝其中一邊的皮，接著再剝另一側的皮，切下幾塊魚片。他靠近船椽，把手放進水裡，水流變得比較不那麼強了。

「他累了，也可能是他在休息，現在我可以吃點海豚肉，休息一會兒，睡個覺。」

p. 76-77 在星光的照耀下，他吃下了其中一塊魚片。

「烹煮過的海豚可真是美味啊！」他說，「不過生的海豚肉味道實在糟透了！我下次決不會沒帶鹽或萊姆就出海。」

空中的雲層正往東方聚集，一顆又一顆他所熟悉的星星漸漸消失蹤影，看來他似乎正往一大片雲層前進，風力也漸漸減弱。

「三、四天後天氣會變得很糟，」他說，「不過幸好不是今晚和明天，老頭子，趁著大魚平穩前進的機會，現在先好好睡一覺吧。」

月亮升起已經好長一段時間了，老人就這麼睡下，大魚穩穩地前進，小船則持續朝雲層形成的隧道前進。老人握著拳頭的右手，突然打到自己臉上，讓他猛然驚醒。握在手中的魚線，讓他的右手掌如烈火灼燒般疼痛，他的左手沒有什麼感覺，但他右手極力拉著魚線，魚線卻還是迅速地滑走。

p. 78-79 終於，他左手感覺到魚線的存在。他往後退，用背抵著魚線，灼燒的刺痛感從背部蔓延至左手，他的左手承受所有的拉力，因而被魚線嚴重地割傷。

就在這時候，大魚猛然衝出海面，又重重地落下，接下來不斷地躍出海面又遁入海中。即使老人不斷地鬆開魚線、還緊緊拉著以免線被扯斷，

但小船依然被拖著急速前進，老人被拖著不得不彎下腰，臉還碰到海豚肉的切片，身體完全不得動彈。

這正是我們等待的時刻，他想，現在就接受挑戰吧！

牠得為這些魚線付出代價，一定得讓牠付出代價。

老人根本看不到大魚在海面上下跳躍，只聽見牠落水時衝擊與水花飛濺的聲音，魚線滑動的速度太快，他的雙

手被割傷得非常嚴重，但是他老早就明白這種事難免會發生。

要是男孩也在，他就可以幫忙打濕幾捲魚線，沒錯，要是男孩在就好了。

魚線不斷地被往外拉，不過大魚的速度漸漸減緩下來，老人盡量讓牠一次只拉走一吋，現在他已經能把頭抬起來，臉頰也不必一直被魚片貼著摩擦，原本他是跪在船上，現在他試著站起身，他還是持續放開魚線，但每一次都會縮短放手的長度。

p. 80-81 不知道是什麼原因讓牠突然做出這些舉動，是飢餓讓牠感到絕望嗎？還是夜裡的什麼東西嚇到牠了？

也許是牠突然感到恐懼？但這是一條冷靜又強壯的大魚，何況牠似乎毫無畏懼又充滿自信，實在是太奇怪了。

「你自己最好也是無所畏懼、充滿自信啊，老頭子。」他對自己說道。

老人用左手拉著魚線，彎下身用右手舀了點海水，把剛剛被壓在臉上擠爛的海豚肉給洗掉，他擔心這些魚肉會讓他反胃，讓他吐出吃過的食物導致身體失去力量。他用海水洗淨右手，接著便一直將手放在鹹鹹的海水裡，看著日出前的第一道光芒。大魚似乎是朝著東方前進，他想，那代表牠覺得累了，因此隨著海流的漂浮，接著牠會開始打轉，然後我們的工作才真正開始。

等他覺得右手在水裡泡得差不多了，便把手縮回來瞧一瞧。

「看起來還不錯，」他說，「反正疼痛對一個男人來說根本不算回事。」

他小心翼翼握著魚線，以免傷口又被線碰到，接著他移動身體的重心，從小船的另一側把左手也放進海水中。

p. 82-83 「對沒什麼用處的東西來說，你剛剛的表現還不算太糟，」老人對自己的左手說道，「不過我有段時間的確對你很失望。」

為什麼我的兩隻手生來會不一樣優秀呢？他想，或許是我自己的問題，沒有好好鍛鍊我的左手，不過上帝可鑑，它過去學習的機會可不少，況且它昨晚的表現也並不是那麼差，只有抽筋一次。要是它又抽筋的話，就讓魚線把它割斷算了。

自老人出海以來，這已經是第三次日出了，而正當日出時，大魚開始在水中繞圈。

「牠繞圈的範圍很大，」他說，「但是牠的確是在繞圈沒錯。」

我得盡可能握緊魚線，老人心想，拉力會縮短牠每次繞行的距離，說不定不到一小時我就能看到牠浮出水面了，現在我要先說服牠，接下來就殺了牠。

但是大魚就這麼慢慢地繞著圈，而兩小時後，老人全身都被汗水濕透，他已經累得筋疲力竭。所幸現在大魚繞的圈子短多了，而且從魚線傾斜的角度來看，他可以判斷大魚穩定地往上接近水面。

大約有一小時的時間，老人眼前不斷看到黑點，汗水刺痛他的雙眼及眼睛下方和額頭的傷口；對於眼前那些黑點他並不擔心，但是他卻連續兩次覺得暈眩甚至要昏倒，這反而讓他感到憂心。

p. 84-85 「我不能失敗，不能像這樣死在一條魚的手上，」他說，「如今這麼棒的一條大魚來到我面前，上帝幫助我忍下來，我會多唸一百次慈愛的天父與聖母瑪麗亞，雖然現在我沒辦法唸出來。」

就假裝我已經唸過了吧，他想，反正我以後會唸的。

這時他感到手中的魚線一陣重重的拉扯，又快又猛。

一定是大魚在想辦法攻擊魚線，老人心想，牠可能會猛力跳躍，不過現在我寧願牠繼續在水裡繞圈子，牠必須躍出水面才能呼吸新鮮的空氣，但是牠每跳一次，都會加大魚鉤所弄出的傷口，反而讓牠能掙脫魚鉤。

「別跳啊，魚兒，」老人說，「千萬別跳！」

大魚又撞擊了魚線好幾次，每一次老人都放出一小段魚線。

過了一陣子，大魚不再攻擊魚線，又開始緩慢地在水中繞行，這時老人持續緩慢地拉回一些魚線，但卻又開始覺得暈眩，他用左手舀了些海水潑在臉上，接著又多潑了一些，並搓揉了酸痛的後頸。

「我現在已經不再抽筋了，」他說，「牠很快會再浮上來，而我還是可以支撐下去。你一定得撐下去，這點根本不用再提。」

這時老人背靠著船首跪下休息一會兒，再次將魚線環繞至背部。我要趁著牠繞圈轉的時候先休息一下，等牠浮上來再站起身好好對付牠，他決定了。

p. 86-87 我從來沒這麼累過，他想，而且現在開始吹起季風了，他可以靠這陣風把牠捕上來。海水已經隨風漲高，不過這是一陣輕柔舒適的微風，而且他還得靠這陣風返航回家呢。

「現在我要往西南方前進，」他說，「人是不會在海上迷路的，況且我住的地方還是個很長的島嶼。」

一直到大魚轉到第三圈時，老人才初次看到牠，他看到的是在船下深色的影子，影子很長，小船花不少時間才通過牠整個身體，老人不敢相信這條魚會有這麼長。

「不可能，」他說，「牠不可能會這麼大。」但牠的確就是那麼大，這一圈繞到最後，大魚漸漸接近水面，距離小船大約只有三十碼，老人看見牠浮在水面上的尾巴，比大鐮刀的刀柄還要長，尾巴在深藍色的水面上，呈現淺紫色的色澤。

大魚就在水面下游著，老人能清楚地看見牠龐大的體積與皮膚上的紫色條紋，牠的背鰭往下彎曲，巨大的胸鰭向外擴張，接著老人見到了牠的眼睛。

現在老人不停地冒汗，但卻不是因為陽光的照耀，每當大魚平靜地繞完一圈，他就收回一些魚線，他很確定只要大魚再繞兩圈，他就有機會把魚叉刺向牠。

p. 88-89 但是我得讓牠接近一點，再接近一點，他想，我絕不能刺牠的頭，一定得命中心臟。

「冷靜一點，堅強一點，老頭子。」他對自己說。

大魚在這一圈中往小船的方向游過去，只平靜而優美地擺動魚尾，老人拉著魚線想把牠拉得更近一點，就在那一瞬間，大魚稍微往他那裡移動了方向，接著牠把身子調直，又繼續繞另一個圈。

「我拉動牠了！」老人說，「我剛才讓牠轉向了！」

這時他又開始覺得暈眩，但是還是使勁拉著魚線控制住大魚，我拉動牠了，他想，說不定這一次我就能解決牠了。用力拉吧，雙手，他想，站穩吧，雙腿！我的頭腦啊，為了我撐下去吧，這一次我一定要把牠給拉上來。

但是就在他傾全力往前拉的時候，大魚轉了個方向又游走了。

「魚啊！」老人說，「魚啊，反正你一定得死的，難道要拖著我一起走嗎？」

p. 90-91 這樣下去什麼事也做不了，他想。他口乾得要命，連話都沒辦法說，但是現在他的手根本沒辦法拿到水。他心想，這次我一定要把牠拉到船邊，牠繞太多圈我的技術就不行了，不會的，他告訴自己，你的技術一直都是這麼好。

繞到下一圈時，他幾乎要抓到牠了，不過又一次，大魚調整方向，慢慢地游開。

你這是在害死我啊，大魚，不過你絕對有權這麼做，

171

我過去從未見過比你更大、更美、更冷靜、更高貴的生物，朋友。來吧，結束我的性命！我不在乎是誰殺了誰。現在你自己的腦袋都糊塗了，老頭子，老人心想，你得讓自己的頭腦保持清醒，知道如何像個男人或是像條魚一樣忍受折磨。

「清醒一點，頭腦。」他的聲音小到自己都幾乎聽不見，「清醒一點。」

接著他又再試了一次，當他試著改變大魚行進的方向，他感覺到自己變得更加虛弱，大魚又變換了方向，在空中緩緩揮動著巨大的魚尾，往別的方向游去。

我一定要再試一次，老人對自己承諾道，雖然他的雙手早就軟弱無力，視力也模糊不清。

p. 94-95

[第五章] 鯊魚攻擊

老人忍受著身上的一切痛苦，用他僅剩的力量、他消失已久的自傲，凝聚成一股力量，奮力與大魚抵抗。

大魚游到小船邊，緩緩游著，正要經過小船。

老人把魚線拋在船上用腳踩著，拿起魚叉盡可能把它高高舉起，用盡全身力量一把插進大魚胸鰭的後方，他感覺到鐵叉刺進魚身，他把身體緊貼著魚叉，使勁把鐵叉刺向更深處，再用全身的力量猛推。

接著大魚突然猛力掙扎，牠體內因死亡的威脅，從水中高高躍起，展現牠驚人的身長與寬度，展現牠的力量與美麗；整個情景看起來牠彷彿是高掛在老人與小船的上空，接著牠重重地落入水中，激起一大片浪花。

p. 96-97 老人覺得暈眩反胃，眼睛也看不清楚，不過他拿掉魚叉上的魚線，讓魚線慢慢滑過滿是傷痕的雙手，當他的視線不再模糊時，他看見大魚翻著銀亮的魚肚浮在水面。魚叉的尖端整個刺穿大魚的肩部，從心臟流出的鮮血染紅了整片海水，魚身銀亮，靜靜地隨著海流漂浮，老人把頭埋進雙手裡。

「保持頭腦清醒吧！」他說，「我是個疲累不堪的年邁老頭，但我還是殺了這條我視為兄弟的大魚，現在我得開始做費力的工作。」

我要先把拉繩準備好，把牠綁在小船邊，他想，小船根本載不動牠。

老人先把大魚拉到小船邊，我想看看牠，他想，摸摸牠、感受牠的存在。如今牠是財產了，老人心想，但這不是我想碰牠的原因。我第二次用魚叉刺牠的時候，似乎感覺到了牠的心跳。現在就把牠拉過來，先用繩索套住魚尾，再用繩子的另一端套住魚身，綁在小船邊。

p. 98-99 「開始工作吧，老頭子！」老人說，喝了小小一口水。

「戰役結束了，從現在起淨是些用勞力的工作。」

他抬頭看看天空，再將視線移到大魚身上。

「過來吧，魚兒！」他說，當然大魚沒有過來，只靜靜躺在水面上，老人便將小船划向牠。

當大魚的頭抵到船首時，老人簡直不敢相信牠有那麼大。

「那的確是唯一能殺了牠的方法。」老人說。現在他覺得舒服多了，頭腦也變得清醒。牠一定超過一千五百磅，他想，說不定還更重呢。

「我想偉大的狄馬喬絕對會對我今日的表現感到驕傲。」

他將大魚緊緊綁在小船邊，從船尾一直到中間座板的部分，牠的體積實在太大了，簡直就像是在小船邊綁了另一艘大船一樣。他能夠看見大魚的存在，只要看看自己的雙手、感覺到靠著船尾的背部，他就知道剛剛的那一幕的確有發生，而不是一場夢。

p. 100　小船和大魚平行綁在一起，共同往前航行，老人心想，就讓牠拉著我走吧，如果這能讓牠高興的話，我唯一勝過牠的不過是比較會耍詭計，況且牠現在也傷害不了我。

這是第一隻鯊魚攻擊的前一個小時，當大魚身上一大片暗紅的血液沈下海、在海面下好幾哩處擴散，鯊魚也從深海中游上來。鯊魚游動的速度如此之快，整個海面在陽光下濺起一片藍色浪花，接著牠沒入海水中，隨著血腥的氣味，開始跟在小船和大魚後方。

p. 102-103　有時候鯊魚會追丟這股血腥味，但是牠很快又會找到，然後游得更快更猛。這是一隻鮫鯊，游動的速度居海中生物之冠。牠全身都很美，只除了那一張嘴。牠的背部和旗魚一樣藍，魚肚銀亮，外皮光滑美好，在上下顎間的八排牙齒全往內傾斜，牠的牙齒並不像一般鯊魚一樣，是尖銳的金字塔型，而是像人們彎曲如爪子般的手指，每一顆牙齒幾乎都和老人的手指一樣長，而且兩端都有如剃刀般尖利的切面。

當老人見到鯊魚迎面而來，他立刻明白這隻鯊魚無所畏懼，絕對會極力達到牠的目的。看著鯊魚接近，他也一邊把魚叉和繩子準備好。

如今老人的頭腦清醒，也充滿決心，但獲勝的機會卻不大，好事總是不能維持到最後，他想。

當然這一切可能只是一場夢，我沒辦法讓牠不攻擊我，但是我說不定能捉到牠，你這牙尖嘴利的鯊魚，老人想，去你媽的！

p. 104-105 當鯊魚對著大魚攻擊時，老人看到牠張開大口，閃著奇特的眼神，就在牠撕扯大魚尾部的肉時，他甚至聽見牙齒碰撞、清脆的喀嚓聲。這時他將魚叉猛力刺往鯊魚頭部，再用力推進腦中，他用自己布滿鮮血的雙手對鯊魚展開攻擊，用盡全身的力量把魚叉刺向鯊魚。他對這次攻擊不抱希望，但下手時充滿要傷害牠的決心。

鯊魚在水面上擺盪，老人發現牠的眼神不再有生氣，他明白鯊魚馬上要喪失性命。但牠的意志不願接受這樣的事實，牠在海面上猶如快艇般急速前進，接著在海面漂浮了一陣便緩緩沈入深海中。

「牠大概吃掉了我40磅的魚肉，還帶走了我的魚叉。」老人說道。他不願轉頭望向那條大魚，牠的身體已殘破不完整，當鯊魚攻擊牠時，老人感覺就彷彿是自己被攻擊。

好事總是無法長久，他想。如今真希望這一切只是一場夢，希望我從沒釣到那條魚，而是獨自躺在鋪著報紙的床上。

「但是一個人可不是生下來被打敗的，」他說，「一個人可以被毀滅，但決不能被擊敗。」雖然我很難過殺了那條魚，他想，現在艱難的時刻來臨了，我甚至連魚叉都沒了。

「別想了，老頭子。」他大聲地說著，「繼續航行下去吧，無論發生什麼事都要接受。」

p. 106-107 他心裡其實明白得很，等小船划到洋流內會發生什麼事，不過目前還不太需要做什麼準備。

「不對，還是有的，」他高聲說，「我可以把刀子綁

175

在其中一支船槳的尾端。」

接著他也這麼做了。

「現在，我還是個老頭子，但是不再毫無防禦能力了。」

他看著大魚身軀的前半部，感覺又有了一些希望。

要是不心懷希望的話實在太傻了，他想，我相信這絕對是一種罪惡，還是先別想到罪惡吧，眼前的麻煩已經夠多了。

我對宗教上的罪行一無所知，況且我也不確定自己相不相信。說不定殺魚便是一種罪惡，雖然我這麼做是為了謀生，也餵飽了很多人；但如果這是一種罪惡，那麼一切行為不也都是嗎？別再想犯罪了吧，你生來就是個漁夫。

你殺了那條大魚並不只是為了保住性命，不只是為了販賣換取糧食，他想，你殺牠是為了榮譽，是因為你本來就是一名漁夫。牠活著的時候你敬愛牠，牠死後還是一樣，如果你敬愛牠，那麼殺牠就不是一種罪惡，或者這是一種更嚴重的罪行？

但是你殺那條鮫鯊時卻樂在其中，他想。

「我殺牠是為了自衛，」老人大聲喊著，「我殺牠並非是不恰當的作法。」

況且就某方面來說，生物不就是彼此互相殘殺嗎？捕魚會讓我喪失性命，一如它也能讓我繼續活下去，小男孩讓我想活下去，我就別再騙自己了吧。

p. 108-109

加勒比海

若以面積大小來分類，世界上最大的主要海域，分別是南中國海、地中海與加勒比海。南中國海常出現在現今的新聞標題中，因為中國大陸、越南、馬來西亞和菲律賓，都想要取得這片海域中能源的控制權；地中海在早期西方文明的演進扮演極為重要的角色；至於加勒比海則是因澄淨的海水、美麗的珊瑚和豐富的水上活動而馳名，當然也因爲海明威將《老人與海》的背景設在該海域而著名。

　　喜愛釣魚、潛水，或是想躺在白色沙灘放鬆身心、在清澈海水中游泳的遊客，都將加勒比海視爲最佳景點，這裡有許多島嶼過去都是歐洲國家的殖民地，古巴是其中最大的島嶼，其獨特之處在於它也是現今依然存在的共產國家之一。古巴的首都，哈瓦那，也出現在海明威的故事中，這個首都曾是著名的觀光景點，許多富有或出名的美國人過去常來這裡度假，但自從古巴被社會主義的政府控制後，哈瓦那對遊客已無過去的吸引力了。

p. 110-111

[第6章] 最後的戰役

　　老人繼續航行兩小時後，又遇見另外兩條鯊魚的其中一條。

　　「鯊魚！」他大喊著。

　　他拿起纏著刀子的船槳，盡可能不用太大的力氣，因爲他的手本能地反抗這股痛苦，他只能看著鯊魚往前逼近。

　　牠們是兇狠惹人厭的鯊魚，是氣味難聞的清道夫，是無情的殺手。當牠們難忍飢餓時，甚至會一口咬下船槳或是船舵。

　　「好啊！」老人說，「來吧，鯊魚！」

　　牠們眞的過來了，一隻轉向，游到小船下方不見蹤影，老人感覺小船一陣搖晃，其實是鯊魚在猛力拉扯大魚。另一隻鯊魚用牠黃澄的大眼瞪著老人，接著便火速游向大魚，攻擊牠原本被咬過的部分。在鯊魚呈棕色的頭上有條清楚的線，一直延伸至後腦與脊髓交界處，老人將綁在船槳上的刀刺向鯊魚的腦袋，把刀抽回來，又再刺向鯊魚如貓一般的黃色雙眼。鯊魚放開口中的大魚，溜進海底，在死前把先前咬下的魚肉吞下肚裡。

p. 112-113 老人見到另一隻鯊魚，連忙靠過去對牠猛力一擊，這次猛擊讓他傷了雙手和肩膀，但是很快地鯊魚把頭冒出水面，又迅速游了過來，老人毫不遲疑便往牠平坦的頭頂刺下去，拔回刀子，再往同一個地方攻擊。接著老人用刀猛刺鯊魚的左眼，但是鯊魚依然不動如山。

「不肯走嗎？」老人說著，把刀刃刺向鯊魚的脊椎和腦袋間，感覺到牠的軟骨被他刺破了！

「走吧，鯊魚，沈到一哩以下的深海中，去陪伴你的朋友吧！或者那隻是你母親？」

老人擦拭著刀鋒，把船槳放下，讓小船返回正確的航向。

p. 114-115 「牠們想必吃掉這條大魚的四分之一了，還都是魚肉的最佳部位。」他大聲說道，「真希望這一切只是一場夢，這條大魚根本就沒有上鉤，我為此感到難過，魚兒啊，一切都變調了。」他停頓下來，不願再看大魚一眼。

「我根本就不應該跑來這麼遠的地方，大魚，」他說，「無論是你或是我，都不應該。我很抱歉，大魚。天知道最後那條鯊魚吃了多少魚肉，」他繼續說道，「不過小船的確輕了很多，」他根本不敢去想大魚下方到底被咬得多狼狽。

這條魚大到可以讓一個男人撐一整個冬天，老人想。別再想這些了，休息一下，讓雙手恢復正常，好好保護你剩下的魚肉吧！

接下來出現的是一隻單獨行動的鏟鼻鯊。牠看起來像一隻走近飼料槽的豬，嘴巴大得人都可以把頭伸進去。老人讓牠攻擊大魚，接著用船槳上的尖刀一刀刺向牠的腦袋，但是鯊魚翻了一圈便往後猛退，刀刃也應聲折斷。

老人甚至不再看著緩緩沈入水中的情景。

「我還有個魚鉤，」他說，「不過這用不上，我還有兩支船槳、一把舵柄和一根短棍。」

牠們擊敗我了，他想，我實在太老，沒辦法把鯊魚給打死，但是只要我還有這有兩支船槳、舵柄和短棍，我就會繼續拚下去。

p. 116-117 現在時間已接近傍晚，但是老人眼前除了海洋與天空，其他什麼也看不到。

「你累了，老頭子！」他說，「你的內心覺得厭倦了。」一直到日落前，都沒有鯊魚來攻擊小船。

他撐住舵柄，跑到船尾下方把短棍拿出來，那原本是斷裂船槳的握柄，兩隻鯊魚同時朝小船逼進，比較接近的一隻張開血盆大口，上下顎深深陷在大魚銀色的外皮上，老人高高舉起短棍，往鯊魚寬闊的頭頂奮力敲下。鯊魚從大魚身邊下沈，老人又猛力敲擊牠的鼻尖。

這時另一隻鯊魚也張開大口再次進攻，老人見到好幾塊魚肉從牠嘴邊露出，他這次只對著鯊魚的頭部重擊，鯊魚看著他，依然撕扯著魚肉，老人再次拿短棍揮向牠。

「來啊，鯊魚，」老人說，「再來啊！」

p. 118-119 鯊魚果然往前逼近，老人趁牠閉上嘴時再次攻擊，他盡可能把棍子抬高，使盡力氣敲向鯊魚，這次他甚至能感覺自己擊中牠的骨頭，接著便往同一個地方猛擊。老人繼續警覺地看著，但是再也沒有鯊魚回來攻擊。

現在老人根本不想再看大魚了，他心裡明白牠一半以上的體積都被摧毀了，而在他與鯊魚奮戰的同時，太陽也已經下山了。

「馬上就要天黑了，」他說，「接下來我應該能看見閃著金光的哈瓦那海灘，如果我已經偏離東方太遠，那麼我應該會見到某個新海灘上的陽光。」

現在他無法再與大魚對話，牠已經被攻擊得體無完膚。接著一個想法閃過他腦中。

「你這半隻魚呀，」他說，「你之前還是一條完整的魚，很遺憾我航行得太遠，把我們倆都給害慘了，不過我們的確殺了不少鯊魚啊，你和我一起幹掉了不少魚。你以殺過多少魚啊，老魚？你那張尖利的嘴可不是白長的吧！」

現在我還有半條魚，他想，說不定我夠幸運，能把這半條帶回去，我應該還有點運氣吧？不對，他說，你把小船划得太遠，把運氣都給用完了。

「別傻了，」他高聲地說道，「說不定你還有點運氣，要是有地方在賣好運的話，我可要去買一點。」他說。

p. 120-121 但是我能用什麼來買呢？難道我能用壞掉的魚鉤、折斷的刀子來買嗎？還是用我這兩隻沒用的手？

「說不定你真的可以，」他說，「你在海上待了八十四天就是為了買一點運氣，而他們也差一點就賣給你了。」大約晚間十點左右，他看到了城鎮反射出耀眼的光芒，他朝著亮光的中心駛過去，心中想著，再過不久應該就能抵達小溪邊了。

現在一切都結束了，老人心想，牠們可能會再度來攻擊，但在這片黑暗中，一個手無寸鐵的人又能怎麼對付牠們呢？真希望我不必再應付牠們，老人想著。

但是到了午夜時分，他依然得對付鯊魚，然而他知道這將是一次無謂的對抗。牠們成群結隊而來，他只能絕望地聽聲音、憑感覺地胡亂攻擊，突然間他感覺有某樣東西奪走了他手中的棍子，他鬆開船尾的舵柄，兩手緊緊握住，一次又一次盲目地敲打攻擊。

p. 122-123 最後，一條鯊魚逼近大魚頭部，奮力搶食，老人知道一切都已結束，他拿著舵柄揮向鯊魚頭部，一次、一次、又一次。鯊魚終於放開，翻滾著游開，這是那群鯊魚中的最後一隻，而且大魚身上再也找不到任何殘餘的肉能餵飽牠們了。

現在老人連呼吸都覺得困難，嘴裡還有種怪異的味道，像是銅與甜味的混合，有那麼一瞬間他無法忍受這股味道，於是朝海水裡啐了一口，說著：「嚐嚐這個吧，鯊魚！」

他知道自己最終依然被擊敗，輸得徹徹底底，他把麻布袋扛在肩上，將小船划向正確的航線，現在他無法思考，也毫無感覺，唯一注意到的就是小船航行地多麼輕巧順利，因為已經沒有太大的重量阻礙它前進。

他感覺到目前正順著洋流前進，也已經看見岸邊的燈光。

p. 124-125 當船駛進小港灣裡，露臺酒館的燈光已經熄滅，所有人都已經睡了。他將小船拉上岸，跨步下船，再把它綁在岩石邊。接著他把船桅卸下，捲起帆布後綁好，將船桅扛在肩上開始往上爬，直到現在他才明白自己有多疲累。這時他停下腳步，回過頭看著大魚潔白光滑的背脊、顏色深黑帶著尖喙的頭部，以及中間只剩空殼的骨架。

接著他又開始往上走，走到頂端時跌了一跤，於是便將船桅抵在肩上停下來休息一會兒。接著老人努力想站起身，但這對他而言實在太困難了，所以他便坐在那兒，肩上扛著船桅。

終於，他先放下船桅，站起來後再拿起船桅扛在肩上，開始往路上走。在走回他的小屋之前，他不得不停下

來休息了五次。

到了屋裡，他把桅杆放到牆邊，在黑暗中他找到水瓶喝了些水，之後便到床上躺下，拉起毯子蓋住身體，趴在鋪著報紙的床上，雙臂打直手掌朝上地睡了。

清晨，小男孩透過門往屋裡看，老人仍在沈睡中。男孩看到老人的雙手時，哭了起來。他飛快地跑去幫他拿些咖啡，整條路上他都在哭。

p. 126-127 許多漁夫圍在小船邊看著一旁的魚骨，其中一人捲起褲管走進水中，正在測量魚骨的大小。

小男孩並沒有過去，他之前已經去過了，其中一位漁夫在幫他看著魚骨。

「他還好嗎？」一名漁夫喊道。

「他在睡覺，」男孩大聲說，他不在乎讓其他人看到他在哭，「別讓人去打擾他。」

「牠從鼻尖到尾巴總共是十八呎長。」剛剛在測量魚骨的漁夫吼道。

「這我相信。」男孩說。

他走進露臺酒館點了一罐咖啡。

「熱咖啡，加很多牛奶和糖。」

「還要別的嗎？」

「不用了，過一會兒我再看看他能吃些什麼。」

「那到底是什麼魚啊？」酒館老闆問，「過去從沒見過這麼大的魚，幫我跟他說我很抱歉。」

「謝謝。」男孩回道。

p. 128-129 男孩拿著那罐熱咖啡回到老人的小屋，坐在他身邊等他醒過來。

終於，老人醒了。

「別坐起來，」男孩說，「先把這個喝了吧。」他在杯裡倒了些咖啡。

老人接過咖啡喝下。

「牠們擊敗我了，瑪諾里，」老人說，「牠們完完全全地擊敗我了。」

「沒有，那條魚沒有擊敗你。」

「不，我真的被打敗了，是在那條魚之後的事。」

「培利戈在幫你看著小船和釣具，那條魚的頭你想怎麼處理？」

「就讓培利戈切下來做魚餌吧！」

「那魚嘴呢？」

「如果你想要可以留下來。」

「我要，」男孩說，「現在我們要好好計畫其他事了。」

「他們有去找我嗎？」

「當然啦，海岸巡防隊和飛機都出動了。」

<p. 130-131> 「海洋太大了，小船又那麼小，很難找到的。」老人說。現在能有個人說說話，比起在海上自言自語愉快多了。

「我很想念你，」他說，「你捕到了些什麼？」

「第一天和第二天都捕到一條，第三天兩條。」

「很好。」

「從現在起我們又可以一起捕魚了。」

「不行，我運氣不好，我的運氣再也好不起來了。」

「管他什麼運氣！」男孩說，「我自己就會帶來好運。」

「你家人會怎麼說？」

「我才不在乎呢，昨天我就捕了兩條魚，不過我們還是要一起捕魚，因為我還有很多要學，你快把手給治好吧，老先生。」

「我知道要怎麼照顧我的手，昨天晚上我吐了些怪怪的東西，還覺得胸口裡似乎哪裡破了。」

183

「這些也要早點治好，」男孩說，「先躺下來，老先生，我會幫你拿乾淨的襯衫過來，再帶點東西給你吃。」

「給我帶一份我不在這幾天的隨便一份報紙吧。」老人說。

p. 132-133 「你要盡快好起來，我可以學很多很多，你可以把一切都教給我。你到底受了多少罪？」

「很多！」老人說。

「我會幫你帶食物和報紙過來，」男孩說，「好好休息吧，老先生，我會去藥局幫你拿一些治療手的藥。」

當男孩離開門口走到路上，他又哭了起來。

那天下午，露臺酒館為遊客舉辦了一場舞會，一名女子透過空酒瓶和一條梭魚間的空隙，看到又大又長的白色脊骨，巨大的尾部隨著海朝的波動而浮起。

「那是什麼？」她指著大魚長長的背骨問服務生，現在那只是一個等著被潮流沖走的垃圾。

「Tiburon，」服務生說，「是鯊魚！」他試著解釋清楚。

「我以前都不知道鯊魚竟然會有形狀這麼漂亮的尾巴。」

「我也不知道。」她的男伴說道。

回到路上，在他的小屋裡，老人再度睡著了。他還是臉朝下趴著睡，小男孩就坐在他旁邊看著他，這回老人又夢到非洲的那群獅子了。

Answers

p.48   A   ❶ F   ❷ F   ❸ T   ❹ T   ❺ F   ❻ F

        B   ❶ The old man will be hooking a huge fish.
            ❷ The old man will be rowing far out to sea.
            ❸ The tuna fish will be jumping out of the water.

p.49   C   ❷ ⇨ ❺ ⇨ ❶ ⇨ ❸ ⇨ ❹

        D   ❶ trousers   ❷ taut   ❸ current   ❹ made
            ❺ dream

p.92   A   ❶ F   ❷ T   ❸ T   ❹ F   ❺ T

        B   ❶ (b)   ❷ (a)

P.93   C   ❶ fillets   ❷ poured   ❸ as long as
            ❹ strange   ❺ lurch

        D   ❹ ⇨ ❶ ⇨ ❺ ⇨ ❸ ⇨ ❷

P.134   A   ❶ T   ❷ F   ❸ T   ❹ F   ❺ T

        B   ❶ violated   ❷ swallowed   ❸ harbor
            ❹ pack   ❺ jaws

P.135   C   ❶ (b)   ❷ (d)

        D   ❶ − ⓑ   ❷ − ⓐ   ❸ − ©

p.144   A   ❶ All that's left of the fish at the end of the story
              is a skeleton. (T)
           ❷ Joe DiMaggio once spoke to the old man. (F)

❸ The old man has a deep knowledge of the sea and its creatures. (T)

❹ There are many sharks waiting in the current near the shore. (T)

❺ The old man is in terrible physical shape at the end of this book. (T)

❻ The boy thinks he can't learn anything more from the old man. (F)

B **❶** What is this story about? (c)

❷ Why did people call the old man 'The Champion' when he was young? (a)

p.145 **C** **❶** skiff empty   **❷** through this fiction

❸ rowing steadily   **❹** convince, no match

❺ unclear   **❻** faint and sick

D **❶** The old man had to fish alone.

❷ The sharks ate the entire fish before the old man could get it to shore.

❸ The old man hooks into a huge marlin.

❹ The boy's parents thought the old man was unlucky.

❺ The old man finally managed to harpoon the fish.

❹ ⇨ **❶** ⇨ **❸** ⇨ **❺** ⇨ **❷**

Adaptors of "Let's Enjoy Masterpieces!"

Scott Fisher
Michigan State University (Asian Studies)
Seoul National University (MA, Korean Studies)
Ewha Womans University, Graduate School of Translation
and Interpretation, English Professor

David Hwang
Michigan State University (MA, TESOL)
Ewha Womans University, English Chief Instructor,
CEO at EDITUS

Louise Benette
Macquarie University (MA, TESOL)
Sookmyung Women's University, English Instructor

Brian J. Stuart
University of Utah (Mass Communication/Journalism)
Sookmyung Women's University, English Instructor

David Desmond O'Flaherty
University of Carleton (Honors English Literature and
Language)
Kwah-Chun Foreign Language High School,
English Conversation Teacher

Let's Enjoy Masterpieces!
Grade 5 The Old Man and the Sea

First Published September, 2005
Third Printing May, 2008

Author: Ernest Hemingway
Illustrator: Julina Alekcangra
Recording Artists: Michael Yancey, Mary Jones

Printed and distributed by Cosmos Culture Ltd.
Tel: 02-2365-9739
Fax: 02-2365-9835
http://www.icosmos.com.tw